FROZEN

As the night falls, a woman must decide whether to risk her life for the man she loves — or destroy him before a curse rips everything away...

For a year and a half, Olivia Martin has tried to forget Erik Gulbrandr, the glacial man who'd scorched her mouth with a single kiss. But when Olivia finds herself snowbound with Erik on the winter solstice, she discovers that the man who set her body aflame is cursed by abominable needs — and a desire that might destroy them both…

FROZEN

This book is a work of fiction. Names, characters, places, and incidents are the product of the author's imagination or are used fictitiously. Any resemblance to actual events, locales, or persons, living or dead, is coincidental.

meljean@meljeanbrook.com

Cover photo © Jasmina007 — iStockphoto.com
Cover and Interior Design by Meljean Brook

ISBN-13: 978-1490503097

First Edition: September 2014
CreateSpace Independent Publishing Platform

www.MeljeanBrook.com

Learn more at
www.MeljeanBrook.com

A Gathering of Dragons
The Beast of Blackmoor
A Heart of Blood and Ashes
A Touch of Stone and Snow

Coming Next
A Dance of Smoke and Steel

Learn more at
www.MillaVane.com

FROZEN

MELJEAN BROOK

RENOB DOGS

Chapter One

THIS COULDN'T BE THE RIGHT DRIVEWAY. I PULLED
my Jeep onto the shoulder and checked the rear-
view mirror. No one was coming up the snowy
road behind me. I hadn't spotted another car since
leaving the main highway, and the only evidence
that anyone ever came this way were the tire tracks
leading into a few private drives. I'd expected Erik
Gulbrandr's driveway to look the same, but although
my GPS navigator told me to turn right, I didn't see
a paved lane. Only a thick blanket of snow.

I didn't doubt that the lane lay under the snow,
however. The GPS might have miscalculated the
route—it wouldn't have been the first time the
device steered me in the wrong direction—but I

couldn't mistake the wide, winding path cutting through the stand of pines that stretched south toward the mountains.

Great. Of all the driveways along this road, the one I needed was the only one that hadn't been plowed.

I studied the lane and considered my options. The snow was about two feet deep—probably less beneath the shelter of the pine branches. Could my Jeep make it?

Maybe. My rig regularly handled rough terrain. Before starting up this road I'd put the transmission in four-wheel drive and locked traction chains around the tires. But it would only take one drift to bog me down, and I didn't want to risk getting stuck—especially for Erik Gulbrandr. Though he was one of the partners at the engineering firm where I worked, I avoided him whenever possible. This detour hadn't been my idea; I'd only come as a favor to the senior partner—Erik's father—after he had discovered that I planned on visiting my parents' home for the holidays.

Erik will sign the papers and you'll be back on the road within ten minutes, John Gulbrandr had told me. *All in all, it'll only take you an hour out of your way.*

I'd agreed to do it because taking the papers allowed me to leave work mid-afternoon instead of waiting until five o'clock, which would put me ahead of the snowstorm the local weather forecasters had been hyping for the past three days, and also give me an early jump on my week-long vacation and the four-hour drive to my parents' place near Grand Junction. The Gulbrandrs' lodge was on the way, a few miles off the highway about an hour outside of Denver—but I'd already been delayed by traffic, which had made leaving early pointless.

Now it looked like I'd have to take another hour's detour after Christmas. I'd be driving this way again on my way back home. Hopefully Erik would hire someone to plow his lane before then.

I pushed in the clutch and shifted into first gear, then stopped. Crap. I had no idea what documents were in the manila envelope on my passenger seat, or how important they were. But Gulbrandr had also asked me to send them express as soon as I could get to a mail drop, so he probably wouldn't appreciate them sitting around my parents' house for a week. Maybe he'd prefer that I leave the papers somewhere local so that Erik could pick them up.

With a sigh, I dug my phone from my bag. One bar. Off the highway and in the shadow of the mountains, I was surprised to get any reception at all.

Gulbrandr answered on the second ring. I could easily picture him at his desk, a big man with dark hair liberally salted by gray, wearing an engineer's unofficial uniform of a chambray button-down shirt and tan trousers.

"John Gulbrandr here."

My boss didn't waste time on pleasantries. He was nice enough, I supposed, but all business—and that suited me perfectly. I've never been good as socializing, but I've always been damn good at my job.

"It's Olivia Martin, Mr. Gulbrandr. I've just arrived—"

"Is my boy giving you trouble?"

"No." Did he expect trouble? I only expected Erik to freeze me with his glacial stare and politely show me the door. "I haven't seen him yet. The drive hasn't been plowed, and I can't make it up to the house."

"Damn it. Hold on, then. I'll call him on the other extension. He can meet you at your car."

Silence filled the line. I waited, hoping that I wouldn't lose my connection. Hoping that this little detour wouldn't end up taking much longer than one hour.

And hoping I'd get something to eat soon. My stomach had been rumbling since I turned off the highway. The coffee and muffin I'd grabbed for lunch hadn't lasted, but I didn't want one of the protein bars in my bag. I could pick up something in the next town.

From the corner of my eye, I detected a flash of movement within the trees. I peered through the passenger window, searching for another glimpse. Whatever it had been was already out of sight. A deer, probably. Too big to be a rabbit, and nothing else in these woods would move that fast. I was sorry to have missed it, but the view through the window was pretty enough to make up for my slow reaction. The white-capped mountains created a stunning backdrop to the forest. Alongside the road, pine branches hung low, weighed down with snow that seemed to glow in the soft light of the late afternoon sun. No snowstorm yet, though the heavy clouds to the north said that it wasn't far away. Only an hour of daylight remained—and the shadows between the trees were growing deeper. What the hell was Gulbrandr doing on the other line? Surely he'd had enough time to tell his son to get his ass down to the road.

Unless I hadn't heard anything because I'd lost reception.

I pulled the phone away from my ear and glanced at the screen. Still connected. The call time counted away the increasing minutes. When I put it back against my ear, Gulbrandr was talking.

"—can't get through. The lines must be down and I can't reach him on his cell. Do you have a pair of winter boots and a coat with you?"

"Yes." Of course I did. What did that have to do with anything?

"It's only a quarter mile up to the house," Gulbrandr said.

Oh, for Pete's sake. He wanted me to hike there through the snow? *Really?* "Can't I swing by on my way back to Denver next week?"

"Our accountants want those papers filed by the end of the year. And we're cutting it close as it is, what with the closures and delays over the holidays."

Maybe the firm shouldn't have waited until the nineteenth of December to have them signed, then. But I held my tongue. Obviously, it would have to be done.

"All right. I'll head on out."

"I appreciate it. You're a good woman to have around, Martin." A pause followed. He must have

realized how close that comment came to condescension, especially considering that he'd sent me
on an errand that didn't fall under my job descrip-
tion. He quickly amended, "You do good work."

I know I did—but I wasn't usually a messenger
girl. I said good-bye and tossed my phone onto the
passenger seat in a little snit. I wasn't mad at him,
not really. The quarter-mile walk didn't bother me.
But the way I'd pictured this going had just been
shot to crap. I'd intended to drive up to Erik's house,
coolly knock on his front door, and maintain a
disinterested expression as he signed the papers.
Ten minutes later, I'd drive away.

And in that ten-minute period, I was determined *not* to remember how Erik had once kissed
me like a man starving for my taste—then told me
he'd made a mistake.

There was no chance that our encounter
would last only ten minutes now. He would insist
on walking me back to my Jeep, with icy silence
between us. And instead of coolly knocking on the
door, I'd show up looking like a crazy mountain
woman coming in out of the cold.

Goddammit.

I killed the Jeep's engine and reached into the
backseat for my boots. *Did I have them?* Of course

I had them. A million things could go wrong while driving snowy roads in winter, so in addition to boots, a coat, and the long johns in my suitcase, I also had a sleeping bag, a week's worth of dehydrated meals, a few jugs of water, and air-activated hand and foot warmers.

I liked to make plans. When events didn't go according to plan, then I liked to be prepared for anything else.

In my seat, I toed off the ankle boots I'd worn to the office and switched them for a knee-high pair, tucking my jeans into the insulated interior and lacing them up. An orange down-filled vest topped the navy cable-knit sweater I already wore. Outside, the temperature hovered only a few degrees below freezing, so I didn't bother to zip my coat. I tugged a shearling hat down over my ears and pulled on my wool gloves, then glanced into my bag. Spare set of keys, check. A whistle if I became lost. Pepper spray, in case I ran across a cougar or a bear out of hibernation—or worse, a man I didn't know. I threw in extra hand warmers, then the manila envelope addressed to Erik. Slinging the bag over my shoulder, I made certain the Jeep was far enough off the road, then locked the doors.

I hadn't taken more than two steps when my

phone chirped, signaling a text message.

—*Don't worry if you can't call later. I won't expect you home tonight. Mom.*

Disbelief dropped my mouth open. I read the text again, but her failure to mention *why* I'd be gone told me as well as words could have. If it was the storm, she'd have said so. So she must have seen me staying the night with Erik.

God. What had she *seen*?

Heat spread across my cheeks. My mom almost never did anything like this. Despite her uncanny ability to look into the future and see trouble coming, she adhered to a strict "I'm Not Telling" policy, particularly in regards to my older sister's and my futures. She'd only broken her rule a few times that I knew of—once to tell my sister to hide a drunken friend's keys, and once to warn me that a boy I was dating in high school would hit me in a jealous rage after he saw me talking with another guy.

I hadn't believed her. Joey had been one of the sweetest kids I knew. Neither my sister nor I had my mother's ability, but she'd always told us to trust our instincts—and my gut told me that he was a good guy.

But I'd mistaken hormones for instincts. One

night at a friend's party, I grabbed a couple of drinks before making my way into the living room where Joey waited. He'd stared at me with an expression that I couldn't identify, until I realized that he'd seen me chatting with a guy from my Calculus class in the kitchen. I recognized his fury then, and saw his clenched fist—but even though my instincts raised an alarm, I still hadn't *believed* he'd try to punch me.

Until he'd actually swung.

My mom's warning had prepared me. I'd ducked; he'd missed. So I tossed my drink into his face and slammed my knee into his crotch. He'd probably pissed blood for a week, but he never hit me.

Nothing my mother saw was inevitable. If she didn't interfere, events usually progressed as they originally would have. But just because she saw something didn't mean it had to happen.

I wouldn't be staying the night with Erik. She'd completely misread that future.

—*You're SO wrong,* I texted back. *I'll be there.*

I started up the driveway. A few seconds later, her reply came.

—*Just be careful.*

A little shiver ran up my spine. She never said 'be careful' lightly. Coming from someone with her ability, a 'be careful' could drive a person mad worrying about what she'd seen and what was going to happen to them.

My mother hadn't said it to me in fifteen years—since the night of that high school party. One of the reasons I always prepared myself was so she wouldn't worry. She knew I carried all of that stuff in my bag…yet she still told me to be careful?

Slipping the phone into my coat pocket, I returned to the Jeep. A lockbox sat under the passenger seat. I dialed the combination and lifted the lid. Inside, my 9-millimeter pistol lay nestled in gray foam. I made certain the safety was on and tucked the weapon into my bag—right next to a box of condoms.

I didn't plan to use either. But I did like to be prepared.

CHAPTER TWO

THE TEMPERATURE DROPPED A FEW DEGREES WHEN
I entered the shade beneath the pine trees. Cold, but
without any wind adding to the chill, not bitterly so.

About twenty yards on, the driveway curved to
the west, following the path of a frozen creek on the
left. I lost sight of my Jeep. Ahead, another curve
bent south again. Everything was quiet except for
the rhythmic crunch of snow beneath my boots.

I checked whether my mom had sent another
text and saw a 'No Service' indicator. Of course.
She'd known the phones would be out.

That didn't mean I'd be in Erik's bed tonight.

But now I was thinking of it. *Sex with Erik.* His
mouth hot on mine, his rough hands over my skin,

the heavy thrust of his body between my thighs. A familiar coil of heat tightened in my belly. This wasn't the first time I'd imagined being with him.

Once upon a time, I thought it might happen in reality. I'd met him a year and a half ago, when I'd still been working as a project supervisor with D&E, a local construction outfit. During the excavation phase of a small condo project headed by Gulbrandr Engineering, our backhoe ruptured an old gas line that hadn't been marked anywhere on the plans and hadn't been noted in the survey. After locating the main and stopping the leak, I'd suspended all work on site. Then I called the lead engineer on the project and ripped him a new one.

I hadn't been surprised when Erik Gulbrandr had come to the site and took over as lead. The move was pure damage control for their firm. I'd been lucky not to lose any men. Even without injuries, discovering the gas line meant expensive delays. Gulbrandr had a client to answer to and a reputation to protect.

I had been surprised by Erik Gulbrandr himself, though—and more surprised by my reaction to him.

His looks weren't the reason, though I'd have been dead not to notice him. He was gorgeous in that rough, strong-jawed way that some men had, the sort of dark and handsome that would never model clothes in a magazine but would look just right in a firefighter's uniform or in a saddle roping a steer. He stood a head taller than most men I knew, and the pale blue of his eyes fascinated me anew every time I looked at him.

But I'd grown up around construction sites, and almost every crew had that one guy who could draw a second and third look. I knew plenty of men who fit that 'rugged and masculine' mold—though most of them didn't do it half as well as Erik. And I hadn't gotten where I was by panting over hot men. I could appreciate a walking sexual fantasy without letting him affect me or my work.

Erik got under my skin anyway. Right away, he'd scored points when he hadn't talked down to me. It was difficult enough being female in my field—too many men seem obligated to explain basic concepts to me, despite my master's degree in civil engineering and a decade on the job—but my slight build often inspired an additional measure of condescension. It didn't matter that I was strong and as tough as steel; they saw 'female and petite' and mentally filed me away as a girl.

I hadn't detected a hint of that from Erik. He'd

been as angry about the fuckup and as irritated by the delay as I was. In the on-site project trailer, we'd spread the plans across the table and sketched out a fix. By the end of the day, he'd won my respect—no wiggling in any easier, inferior solutions or cutting corners. And I'd liked him. While we worked he had a laser's focus, but over the course of interruptions and coffee breaks, I also discovered that he had an easygoing personality, and his humor had a wicked little edge. The cynical part of me suspected that he'd turned on the charm to help smooth out my anger, and that it was just another facet of damage control. Every other part of me was keenly interested in Erik Gulbrandr—and when his gaze rested on my face and mouth a little longer than necessary, I thought Erik returned that interest.

I'd seen those looks before. I'm not a ravishing beauty, but I've never lacked for male attention. My best feature is my hair, a thick and glossy chestnut that falls to the middle of my back. On the job, however, my hair isn't much help—often confined by a French braid and concealed by a hard hat. When I'm not wearing makeup to enhance my green eyes and plump up my lips, my mirror tells me that I'm on the attractive side of plain…until I smile. It lights up everything and pushes me straight over into pretty.

By the end of the day, I'd been smiling often.

A week passed before I saw him again, though he called every day with updates. He'd finally gotten the new plans approved at the close of business on a Tuesday. As we'd both been unwilling to delay the project any more, he'd brought the plans by D&E's office the same night so that we could go over the changes and work out a new schedule. Around eight, we'd ordered pizza and took a break.

And for the space of about twenty minutes, I stopped thinking about backfill and excavation depths and that damned gas line. He'd asked me how long I'd been with D&E, and I told him that I'd paid for college by flagging in the summers and on night jobs during the school year. I'd learned that he loved the mountains as much as I did, and whether in skis or hiking boots, he couldn't stay away from them. When he'd leaned in and wiped tomato sauce from the corner of my lips, I'd learned that his hands were calloused and warm.

And I'd discovered that he could scorch my mouth with a kiss.

I'd never been kissed like that in my life. I've been kissed hard before, a big hand flat against my back and hauling me up against a firm chest. I've felt the onslaught of arousal, the sudden tightening of my body, that delicious shudder when a man's tongue penetrates my lips and takes possession of my mouth.

I've never been kissed as if he needed it. As if he'd die without it.

And I've never been pushed away, never had a man throw a gruff, "Forget that. It was a mistake," at me before walking out.

I hadn't forgotten it—but I hadn't blamed him, either. It *could* have been a mistake. If we'd slept together, any conflicts on site might have taken an ugly turn. Even a kiss was a bad idea…yet I liked that he hadn't been able to resist.

I wasn't looking for trouble, though. So I'd dialed my attraction back—outwardly, at least. When I'd seen him again, it might as well have been our first meeting. Erik was still easygoing, still showing those flashes of humor, but he was completely focused on the job. I did the same. The project had progressed smoothly, and ten months later, the day after D&E's final pay estimate had been approved, I'd called Erik and asked him to dinner.

His reply? "It's impossible. Goodbye, Miss Martin."

Five abrupt words. He'd hung up before I could respond, and I'd been left staring at my phone with a hollow ache opening up in my gut.

I wasn't heartbroken. I wasn't. I was just... sorry. That had been one hell of a kiss, and nothing I'd learned about him in our frequent meetings afterward made me question my attraction. I'd liked him. A lot. So desire had sharpened into quiet, painful need, and for ten months I'd carried around the hope of picking up where we'd left off. Everything inside of me had been screaming that Erik Gulbrandr would be The One, and that he was just as interested in me as I was in him.

But I'd been wrong. My hormones had been screwing with my instincts again. And after that cold rejection, I'd been determined not to waste any more time on him.

Perhaps I'd have been successful if, two months later, John Gulbrandr hadn't decided to add a construction arm to his firm. He'd offered my bosses at D&E an obscene amount of money and folded the company into Gulbrandr Engineering. I only glanced once at the salary he offered me before I went, too, but the money hadn't been my only reason. At D&E, I couldn't have advanced any further than project supervisor. I loved the construction work, but I had my eye on a position in project development. After ten years of coming in on a job after all of the development work had been completed, I wanted to take a stab at helping to bring the projects to life, and Gulbrandr's firm was big enough to accommodate me.

I'd only hesitated once: when I realized I couldn't avoid seeing Erik again, which didn't fit my plan to forget about him. Then I'd decided the firm was big enough to accommodate me *and* Erik Gulbrandr.

After that kiss, we'd kept everything between us professional. Surely we could do the same if I took the job at his firm.

So we did. At our first meeting, a hard expression had frozen his features and he'd subjected me to his glacial, penetrating stare—maybe wondering if I'd mention the kiss or give him grief over rejecting the dinner date. But I'd simply offered him my all-business nod, and after a long moment, he'd done the same.

And that had been that. Not an unprofessional look or a touch between us in six months, though we regularly saw each other at the firm's weekly progress meetings. It hadn't taken me long to figure out that his charm and humor *had* been damage control, because I never saw any sign of them again—only that same icy politeness. Erik's coldness had stung at first, but after a while I was grateful for it. In the past few months I'd heard rumors from the engineering division that Erik's temper had been short and hot. I'd never seen evidence of it, but I knew everyone had been tiptoeing around him, and I didn't want to become a target for his anger. So despite my hope to move out of construction, I'd been content to stay in that division a little longer, finishing the projects I'd come into the firm with.

I'd been content…but I hadn't been able to put him out of my mind. Every time I imagined sex, I imagined Erik. I no longer hoped for something happen between us, but I couldn't *stop* myself from noticing him. I was more aware of Erik than I'd ever been aware of any other man. And, by God, I resented that. I resented how I stopped to listen when I heard his name mentioned. I resented how the sound of his voice could start a trembling ache deep inside me. I resented that my attraction hadn't faded—especially because Erik's obviously had.

I resented that it had been so damn easy for him to file me away as a mistake.

But I didn't intend to act on that resentment. My job was worth more to me than that—worth enough to trudge through a quarter mile of snow for, at least. So I would just follow my original plan: knock, get in and out, ten minutes.

I rounded the final bend in the driveway. My steps slowed as I got my first look at the house ahead. Not even a house. More like a castle. A small fortress. Nothing like the Alpine-style lodge that I'd expected.

Granite blocks formed solid walls. At the ground and second levels, the only windows were narrow arrow slits. To my astonishment, a portcullis had been suspended from the gatehouse ceiling. Its sharp spikes dangling over the recessed entrance, where a heavy wooden door waited. Iron bars guarded the full-sized windows in the third story. Two corner towers overlooked the front of the house, each topped by a conical roof. Long icicles hung from the eaves.

Absolutely unreal. I wouldn't have been surprised to see Rapunzel brushing her hair in the turret room. What in the world had possessed the Gulbrandrs to buy—or build—a place like this?

I'd be able to ask him. As I approached the gatehouse, the front door opened and Erik emerged, wearing faded jeans and a gray t-shirt that clung to his broad chest. My stomach clenched at the sight of him, just as it always did.

I resented that, too.

"Olivia?" His voice thunderous, Erik strode out of the shadows within the gatehouse. "What the hell are you doing here?"

My step faltered. That wasn't ice. That was fury.

Erik stopped three yards away. Even at that distance, his height was overwhelming. He stared down at me. His eyes didn't seem glacial now, but burning with hot blue flames.

"Turn around." The words were as rough as gravel. "Get the fuck out of here. *Now.*"

Too stunned to reply, I just shook my head. This wasn't the plan. He'd be coldly polite. I'd be indifferent. I hadn't prepared for anything else.

But I'd been yelled at before. I'd dealt with pissed-off workers, protesters, and neighbors awakened by construction noise. The best response was putting on an impassive expression and explaining my position as evenly as possible.

I withdrew the manila envelope from my bag. "Your dad has papers for you to sign. He said it's important that they're sent out today."

"Fuck my father. Go."

Anger finally boiled through my shock. "I just walked up your goddamn drive to bring these to you." I flung the envelope. It helicoptered toward him and hit his chest before flapping to the ground, one corner embedded in the snow. "So sign them. Then I'll go as fast as I can. Gladly."

My voice shook at the last. Erik's jaw tightened and he glanced up at the sky before closing his eyes. On any other person, his expression might have seemed pleading.

He bent to sweep up the envelope. "Come in, then."

After all that, I didn't want to. He disappeared into the house and I followed slowly, reaction setting in. Though no stranger to conflict, I never liked it. Even when I remained outwardly calm, the adrenaline left me shaky and sick to my stomach. Now that mixed with confusion.

What had I done to deserve that? Maybe his fury wasn't directed at me and I'd just been the unlucky person to show up at the wrong time, but the way he'd ordered me to go had *felt* personal.

And it felt like shit.

With my hands in my coat pockets to conceal their trembling, I stopped just inside the entrance and shut the door. The interior appeared more like what I'd expected from a lodge. A river rock fireplace dominated the great room. The narrow windows allowed only a little sunlight through, but soaring ceilings and knotty pine warmed and opened the space. At a small table in the foyer, Erik had ripped open the envelope and was flipping through the pages, scribbling here and there. His feet were bare, I realized. He'd left wet footprints on the sandstone floor.

He'd gone *outside* without shoes? So stunned by his anger, I hadn't even noticed. Now I looked more closely. He'd walked into the snow with bare feet and a thin t-shirt…and his skin appeared flushed. Perspiration glistened on his forehead and dampened his thick hair.

"Are you sick?"

"Yeah." He gave a hollow laugh. "A fever from hell."

"Shouldn't you be in bed, then?"

He stilled. His fingers gripped the edge of the table. Alarmed that he might topple over, I started toward him. He stopped me with a shake of his head. "Stay back."

All right. I watched him scrawl another signature, my hurt and confusion fading. The reason behind his behavior outside was obvious now—but it didn't excuse him.

"You should have just said you were sick instead

of yelling at me."

"Right. Sorry." Roughly, he stuffed the papers back into the envelope. "I'll kill my father for sending you here."

Erik sounded as if he meant it. No question at whom his anger had been directed—his dad. Maybe I should have expected it.

"He warned me that you might give me a hard time when I asked you to sign those."

"Not because of this agreement. I asked for it."

"Oh." I gave the envelope a dubious look when he held it out. "Are you contagious?"

He smiled without humor. "No."

Maybe not, but I still thought of the hand sanitizer in my bag. It would be rude to use it now, though. I'd wait until I returned to the Jeep. Until then, my gloves would do.

I tucked the envelope away. God, he looked like hell. Flushed and sweating and his entire body tense, as if warding away a trembling case of the chills.

I hesitated. "Do you need anything before I go?"

"No." He yanked open the door and stood with his fingers clamped on the edge. "Just get out of here. Now."

Some men were babies when they were sick.

Apparently Erik was a jackass. I gave him a little salute. "All right. Have a good holiday, then."

He didn't look down at me or answer. With jaw clenched, he stared out through the gatehouse and into the woods.

Great. Don't even say good-bye or wish me a Merry Christmas. Jerk.

Erik flinched as I passed him, his big body stiffening and pulling away from me. Jesus. Like *I* was contagious. Chin high, I walked through the doorway and into the cold.

The door slammed behind me. I glanced back and stopped in my tracks. Erik had followed me out, his eyebrows drawn and his mouth compressed into a hard line.

His eyes still burned with fever. "I'll walk you down."

"Don't be an idiot. You're sick. I can manage."

He apparently didn't agree. When I emerged from the gatehouse and into the snow, he came after me.

God. "Erik, you aren't even wearing shoes."

That made him pause. He glanced at his bare feet. "Wait here."

This was stupid. And I was stupider for waiting. My patience thinned when he returned a minute later wearing a pair of insulated boots, but with the laces untied. Snow would get inside those on his first step. That wasn't the worst of it, though.

I gave him a tight smile. "And your coat?"

He shook his head. "I'm too hot as it is."

Wasn't that a big fat clue to stay home? I stared him down with my best 'you're being ridiculous' expression, but his gaze held mine without flinching.

He extended his hand. "Give me your bag to carry. It always looks so damn heavy."

"It is," I said. "And no thanks. I might not have your giant muscles, but I can handle it."

"I know you can. But there's no reason to—"

"Since when isn't 'no' enough, dammit?"

He reacted as if I'd slapped him. His face stilled and the edges of his mouth whitened. His gaze turned glacial again. Withdrawing his hand, he dragged his fingers through his hair. "'No' is enough," he said gruffly. "So let's get you out of here."

We started off. The icy silence that I'd expected finally descended between us. If only my head would be as quiet.

How could I drive away, knowing that he was out here sick? What if he passed out on the way back? I was going to end up walking to his house again to make sure he wasn't lying in the snow somewhere, and then he'd insist on walking me back down to the road—like a silly high school game of "No, *you* hang up first" but with a feverish man and a quarter-mile driveway.

Maybe this was why my mom thought that I'd be staying the night: I'd be caring for some sick, stubborn idiot who wouldn't put on his coat.

Why had I assumed her message meant Erik and I would sleep together? My brain had jumped straight to sex with him. Thankfully she could only see the future, not read minds. When I arrived at my parents' house tonight, I could pretend that I'd known he was sick all along.

I *wouldn't* be staying here. But dammit, leaving him like this didn't feel right—especially knowing that he was cut off from outside help if anything happened to him. Maybe I could call someone to check on him after I left. Of course, that wouldn't do any good if they couldn't drive up to the house.

"Your dad said the phone lines were down. Is that why you didn't call for a plow? Do you want me to try when I get back on the road?"

"No." He didn't look at me. "I didn't call for a plow because I don't intend to leave and I didn't want anyone to come."

Including me, obviously. But that didn't make

sense. "I thought you were expecting these papers? You said that you asked for them."

"I didn't know they'd come today. And I didn't expect *you* to bring them. He sure as hell stuck it to me there."

His father had? "What does that mean?"

"He's buying out my partnership."

"In the firm?" I had to stop myself from gaping.

"Yes." A bleak smile touched his lips. "Like I said, I asked for it."

And John Gulbrandr had sent *me* with the agreement that dissolved a business arrangement with his son? He hadn't sent a lawyer or come himself? That wasn't the sort of thing to hand over to just anyone.

But maybe that had been Gulbrandr's point. He'd sent the papers along with someone heading out on her vacation, as if buying out his son was just an afterthought.

I hadn't realized my boss could be such a petty dick. "So what do you plan to do now?"

Erik only shook his head, his mouth set in a grim line. I studied his profile, unease building in my gut. Though no longer sweating or flushed, he looked worse than before. His skin drew tightly across his cheekbones and appeared so pale that the shadows beneath the trees gave him a bluish tinge. In a gesture that I believed meant he'd begun to feel the cold, he'd pushed his hands into his front pockets and hunched his shoulders, but now his posture struck me as the tension of a body in pain. Even as I watched, he hunched over a little more, his hands balling to fists in his jeans.

I slowed, realizing that my mom could have been right. I might not be leaving here tonight. I was beginning to think that I *shouldn't* leave—at least not until I knew he'd be okay.

As I fell behind, he glanced back and faced me, waiting. His eyes burned with that feverish blue flame again, his irises so pale they appeared lit from within.

"Listen," I said. "I can get cell reception on the road. Let me call someone for you. At least have the road plowed so an ambulance can come if you need it. I'll walk you back to the house and wait until it's done."

"You're going now."

His shoulders straightened as he started toward me. His voice was low and dangerous, suggesting that if I didn't agree with him, he'd drag me to my Jeep himself.

Just let him try. "Look, I wouldn't feel right if

I—"

"Fuck feeling right." He stopped within an arm's length, and despite his blue-tinged lips and skin, I felt heat radiating from him. How could that be possible? It definitely couldn't be healthy. "All that matters is that you get out of here."

I shook my head. "I know this won't make any sense, but I think I'm supposed to stay here tonight. I think that something bad will happen if I don't."

A tortured look passed over his features. He closed his eyes. "Something bad will happen if you *do*."

If that were true, my mother would have sent me running. She'd only told me to be careful.

"What will happen?" When he didn't answer, I pointed out the obvious. "You're *really* sick, Erik. Why would you risk yourself like this just to get me out of here?"

"I'd do anything to get you out of here." He opened his eyes, his expression suddenly cold and remote. "Do you know why my father sent those papers with you? It's because I told him that he had to make a choice: either I leave the firm—or *you* do."

My heart dropped. "What?"

"I left to get away from you, Olivia." Each word was succinct, like a shard of broken glass. "I can't stand being around you. Now do you still want to stay here with me?"

"No," I whispered, and even that was an effort. My chest felt as if it had been ripped open. I wanted fury to come, to tell him how fucking cruel saying that had been, but the anger couldn't get past the pain.

An unreadable emotion darkened his gaze before he turned. His shoulders hunched again and he plowed through the snow at a quicker pace. In a hurry to get rid of me.

Now I was in a hurry to go. Tucking my chin down, I started after him, stupid questions crowding my head.

Why had he asked his dad to fire me—and why would he leave over it? Was my presence some kind of insult to him? Was my work not up to par? Had I been disruptive in the office? Was it because I'd asked him out—or because I'd kissed him back? Was I just that disgusting?

No. Anger finally caught up to the hurt. I wasn't any of those things. Whatever Erik's problem with me was, it was *his* fucking problem. I hadn't done a damn thing wrong.

Despite knowing that, I also knew that I wouldn't get more than a mile in my Jeep before

I had to pull over and bawl my eyes out. The ache in my throat was choking me. I walked faster. The last thing I wanted was to start crying now. I just needed to get away.

Almost there. I just had to hold it together through one final bend in the driveway and then twenty more yards.

Ahead of me, Erik came to an abrupt halt. A rough, low sound came from him, a wordless denial. Frowning, I drew even and peered up at his face. He was staring toward the main road, his features a desolate mask. I followed his gaze to the end of the driveway, where my Jeep waited. Astonishment rooted me to the spot.

I wasn't going anywhere.

The hood had been torn away from the engine and flung against a tree, where it leaned against the trunk, half-crumpled. At the front of the vehicle, shredded wires and tubing hung over the radiator grill. I recognized the black box of my battery lying in the snow. My tires were flat—the rubber slashed—and it looked as if someone had taken an axe to the door panels and windows.

No, not an axe...unless it had four parallel blades. But those *couldn't* be claw marks. I needed a closer look.

I started forward. Erik's hand shot out and snared my wrist.

"Don't." Protectively, he tugged me back against his side. I glanced up in surprise, but he wasn't looking at me. His gaze searched the shadows between the trees. "We'll return to the house."

Even though he couldn't stand being around me? But I wasn't going to argue. Fear had begun to steal its way through my astonishment and hurt. A fluttering movement caught my eye. My heart jumped and I looked toward the road again. Flimsy pink fabric lifted on a breeze before settling onto the snow.

My nightgown. The rest of my clothes had been strewn about, too—or tossed up into the trees. The red dress I'd planned to wear during Christmas dinner hung from a branch by its halterneck.

But it didn't just hang there. It had been *hanged*.

I stepped back. "Erik?"

He stood frozen beside me, his fingers wrapped around my wrist. I edged closer to him. His big body shuddered, then he released my wrist and slid his arm around my waist, urging me back toward the house.

"Let's go."

I obeyed the gruff command without question,

thinking of his fortress's thick stone walls. I'd be glad to be inside those. "What did that? A bear?"

Though I didn't really think a bear could do that to my rig and my clothes. Maybe a rabid bear cranked up on cocaine, steroids, and gamma rays from space.

"Not a bear." The firm pressure of his arm against my back increased. "Faster, Olivia."

I was already bucking as hard as I could through the snow, my breath burning in my lungs. "I can't go any faster."

"Then give me your bag."

A dead weight on my shoulder. Panting, I nodded. "Okay—"

The world dropped out from beneath my feet. I cried out in surprise, clinging to the strong arm around my waist. Solid heat surged against my side. Erik's chest. He'd swept me up—was carrying me.

Sick with fever and bearing my weight. "You can't—"

"I can because I'm not carrying you. I'm carrying your goddamn bag. You're just attached to it."

My laugh was too loud, my emotions crashing together in a chaotic wreck. Only a few minutes ago, he'd stabbed me with words and now here I was, grateful for his arms around me and my fear sliding away because of the safety his embrace promised.

But it wasn't safe for me here. I might start hoping for something I couldn't have and he obviously didn't want to give.

I looked down as his hands tightened. My breath froze in my chest, killing my laughter. The storm of conflicting emotions died with it, replaced by sheer disbelief.

The skin stretched over the sculpted muscles of his bare arms was a pale, glacial blue. That wasn't a trick of light and shadow—it was *blue*. Sharp claws resembling shards of ice tipped his long fingers. And he wasn't jogging through the snow so much as skimming over the soft surface, as if he stood on an invisible snowboard.

Heart pounding, I dragged my gaze to his face. More pale blue skin, his thick hair a bluish-black and dusted with glittering frost. His jaw muscles bunched as if he were gritting his teeth, then his blue lips drew back and I saw those teeth were sharper than before—and definitely not human.

Or I'd just gone completely crazy. "Erik?"

"Olivia." My name rumbled from him like the muffled roar of an avalanche. "Don't be afraid."

Now I laughed again, because I couldn't do anything else. I heard the hysteria in my voice but couldn't quiet it, then he shifted my weight in his arms and I remembered his icy claws against my thigh and chest. Terror ratcheted my laugh into a scream. I flailed at him, slapping and punching his chest and neck, kicking desperately as I tried to get away.

A clawed hand trapped my wrists. The support beneath my legs disappeared and I dangled two feet off the ground in front of a man I'd kissed and thought I'd known but he was something else, something with diamond chips in his eyes and terrifying teeth in his mouth. His voice thundered, "Olivia, *stop!*"

I slammed my foot between his legs.

The world dropped out from under me again. I fell, landing hard on my back in the snow. The impact knocked the breath from my lungs. Stunned, I lay there, my chest hurting and a tiny bit of sense returning.

Whatever Erik was, he'd been protecting me. Something else had torn apart my rig—and that something might still be around.

With a groan, I rolled over onto my knees, the snow crunching beneath my weight.

"Olivia." Erik rasped my name.

I glanced up. He stood over me, his features

a mask of tension and pain—and almost himself again. Not blue, not his familiar tan, but pale as snow and his gaze burning. He held out his hand. No claws now.

"I'll try to hold it in," he said hoarsely. "But we have to go."

Nodding, I took his hand. He stiffened at my touch and his eyes paled almost to diamond. A tremor shook through him before he drew me to my feet. My gaze searched his face as I rose. "What are you, Erik?"

That bleak smile touched his mouth again. "A man. Mostly."

Now obviously wasn't the time to press for a full answer. "And whatever ripped apart my rig?"

"Also a man…mostly." He pulled me closer, hesitated. "I'll carry you?"

I nodded, remembering the claw marks in the doors of my Jeep. The woods around us no longer seemed beautiful, but dark and ominous, and Erik traveled faster than I did. He swept me up and I linked my arms around his neck.

He started off—not gliding now, but at a brisk jog that reminded me of a soldier's, moving swiftly without compromising awareness of his surroundings. His gaze continually scanned the trees to either side of us. I got my head together and looked over his shoulder, watching our back.

Only trees and snow. Yet I could almost feel something out there, waiting. Relief slipped through me when the house finally came into view. "Do you know who's out there?"

"At least one of the Moon Hound's sons. Maybe more."

That meant nothing to me. "What do they want?"

"To kill me."

I jerked my head back to glance at his face. "*Kill* you?"

"It's a long tradition in our families." His expression darkened. "My father should have known one of them might come soon. But he sent you anyway."

Erik's determination to get rid of me suddenly made more sense. "So you knew this killer would come, and were trying to protect me from him?"

"No." His voice roughened. "I was trying to protect you from *me*. But it's too late for that."

My stomach seemed to hollow out. "What does that mean?"

And from deep within the shadows between the trees, a howl of laughter answered me.

CHAPTER THREE

ERIK ABRUPTLY HALTED, HIS GAZE FIXED TO THE south. His arms constricted around me before he lowered my feet to the ground. With his hand at my waist, he tucked me protectively against his side.

I slipped off my woolen gloves. Never taking my eyes from the trees alongside the driveway, I reached into my bag and withdrew my gun. I thumbed off the safety and held it aimed at the ground in a two-handed grip.

Erik's fingers softly squeezed my waist. I glanced up.

He nodded to the bag. "What else do you have in there?"

"Everything."

Oh, his grin. I hadn't seen that laughing smile in months, but it didn't last long—just a single thump of my heart, then he looked into the woods again. A pair of ravens burst from the treetops, cawing wildly. My gaze followed them up. The sky had darkened. Pink and orange stained the distant clouds. Only a few minutes until sundown.

Beside me, Erik tensed. Shadows moved through the trees ahead. Not just one. At least four or five, slinking along the ground.

"Wolves?" I whispered.

"A few of them are wolves." His hands flexed. Claws sharpened the tips of his fingers again. "But the two giant wolves are really Hounds. So is the one who looks human."

A person? I peered through the dusk and made out a tall figure walking between the slinking shadows—a man.

Mostly, I reminded myself. "So what happens now?"

"You'll run, lock yourself inside my house, and drop the portcullis. I'll stay here and kill the Hounds."

A mocking laugh floated from between the trees. "Kill us, son of Odin's son? Two nights from now will be both a full moon and the winter solstice.

My brothers and I are at our strongest. You should be, as well. We came expecting a fight. We didn't expect to find you at your weakest."

Weak? I'd never associated that word with Erik. But the memory of blue skin and sharp teeth flashed through my mind—of Erik easily dangling me above the ground. Compared to that, perhaps this *was* the weaker version.

He'd changed back because he'd terrified me. I didn't think I'd be so frightened of him now. Quietly, I asked, "Is he saying that because you're holding it in?"

"I'll let it out," Erik said grimly. "You just have to make it into the house first."

The voice from the shadows answered again. "Perhaps you'll kill us, just as you did my eldest brother. But tell her what happens afterward, son of Odin's son. Tell her what your fever is, and how you'll shatter the stone walls to get to her. How you'll find her, no matter where she runs. Tell her of the Ironwood curse."

What *would* happen afterward? *And what curse?* But I wouldn't let the man in the woods make me doubt Erik. Those questions could be answered later. Right now, two things were clear: Erik had been trying to protect me, even from himself; this stranger was trying to terrify me and had ripped apart my Jeep. Deciding which man to trust was a no-brainer.

I raised the barrel of my gun a little. Not aiming at the stranger yet—just letting him know that I was prepared to.

Moving with a silent, predatory stride, the man finally came into view. Silvery hair touched broad shoulders, giving the impression of greater age than his unlined face suggested. In a fitted black silk shirt with the first two buttons undone and tailored trousers, he should have looked out of place—he seemed more 'trendy nightclub' than 'rugged mountain retreat.' But whether because he stood as straight and unyielding as the trees around him, or because something in his direct gaze reminded me of the wolves at his side, he appeared right at home in these snowy woods.

A scrap of pale fabric dangled from his elegant fingers. A handkerchief, I thought, until he brought it to his nose and inhaled.

Not a handkerchief. He held a pair of my panties.

A sickening sense of violation crawled up from my belly. Tearing up my Jeep hadn't been enough. Now he had to threaten me sexually, too.

But I didn't think that I was his real target. The stranger's gaze never left Erik, who stiffened as if absorbing a blow, his body radiating a wave of heat. The bastard was taunting him, I realized—trying to destroy Erik's control.

With his hand at the small of my back, Erik urged me toward the house. "Go."

Fangs gleaming, the wolves snarled. Their yellow eyes fixed on me. They were all big, but two of them were huge—more than twice the size of the others. And the smaller wolves were lean; the two Hounds had wide chests and powerful haunches, with thick furred crests across their shoulders.

I hesitated. If they came after me, I'd rather stand my ground and shoot than turn my back and run.

For the first time, the stranger met my gaze. His nostrils flared. With a frown, he tucked my underwear into his trouser pocket before looking to Erik again. "I can smell the witch's blood in her. You're a fool if you believe it will change anything. She'll never break the curse."

Witch's blood? My confusion only lasted a second.

My mother. She'd never called herself a witch, but I could see how the label fit. Unfortunately, I didn't possess a single hint of magic.

This man didn't need to know that.

"Go, Olivia." Erik's voice had deepened, roughened.

"Why? He's already found me out." I took careful aim and put the first giant wolf in my sights. "I can help you more here."

"You're *both* fools." A sharp grin spread across the stranger's face. "Now my brothers and I will let you reap the consequences, son of Odin's son. Obviously your woman knows nothing of what is to come—and seeing you broken because you've destroyed her will bring us more pleasure than ripping out your throat ever could. Soon you'll beg us to kill you for what you've done."

He walked backward as he spoke, slowly melting into the shadows. The other two Hounds and the smaller wolves followed, except for one. It settled onto its haunches at the edge of the clearing, watching us with a steady yellow gaze.

I didn't lower my weapon. "Did the others really leave?"

"No. But they've gone far enough. Don't put your gun away. Just hold tight." Without warning, Erik swept me up against his chest again. Blue tinged his skin. "And close your eyes."

He wouldn't scare me. Not this time. Though his fingers ended in icy claws, he held me carefully. I suspected that he possessed enough strength to tear me limb from limb, but I felt safe in his arms. He glided across the surface of the snow toward his house...and now I understood why his family owned a small fortress. How often were they threatened?

I glanced back toward the trees, where the wolf still waited, watching us. A real wolf, not one of the Hounds. "Did you really kill their brother?"

"Three years ago, there was another Hound. It might have been their brother. I never had a chance to ask."

"He just attacked you?"

"Yes."

The roughness of his response told me that he didn't want to talk about it further. All right. There was something else just as important to discuss. "What curse was he talking about? What does he think you're going to do to me?"

Whatever it was, Erik thought he might do it, too. *I was trying to protect you from* me.

"Nothing." His arms tightened around me. "Nothing will happen to you."

But the rough determination in his reply didn't

match his expression. I couldn't read the emotion that hardened his features and flattened his gaze, but something deep within me must have recognized it. A despairing, empty ache opened up beneath my breast.

"Erik?" I heard the fear in my voice. What could make him look like that? "What's going to happen?"

He didn't answer immediately, gliding into the gatehouse and setting me down. Slipping my gun into my bag, I waited while he opened the heavy front door. He stepped inside and faced me.

"This raises and lowers the portcullis." Erik reached for an iron lever embedded in the stone wall. Behind me, the gate rattled into place, guarding the entrance. "Keep it down until I return, but be careful. The Hounds are tricksters and shape-shifters. They might conceal themselves, or look like me, or pretend an injury to lure you outside."

"Okay." Keep the Hounds out. Don't be fooled. Got it. "But where are you going?"

"To kill them. Then you'll take my truck and get the hell out of here."

My heart gave a heavy thump. Even though he'd admitted to killing another Hound, I couldn't even begin to process that he would kill the man I'd just seen—and the big wolves, too, which were apparently more Hounds. Brothers.

But Erik didn't wait for it to sink in. He strode into the house, leaving me to stare through the open door after him.

He was going to kill three men. Men who'd threatened us. Who meant to tear out Erik's throat. But there was no one to call for help. The phones were down. The police weren't an option.

I didn't know if the police could do anything, anyway. Not against magic or curses or whatever was going on here. Erik had been supernaturally strong. If the Hounds were a danger to Erik, if they'd torn up my Jeep, they must be strong, too.

So Erik intended to kill them first. To protect us.

Mentally, I could deal with that. Emotionally, I couldn't make it settle. Dread and fear and disbelief roiled sickly through my stomach. It just didn't seem real.

But the wolf sitting at the edge of the clearing looked real enough. When I looked back into the house, the long iron-tipped spear that Erik took from a pair of brackets mounted over the fireplace looked real enough, too.

And it looked old. The weapon's shaft had faded to the palest of grays—except near the spearhead, where black stained the wood.

Blood, I realized. Old blood. From other Hounds, probably.

Oh, God. This was really happening. The realization swept over me, leaving me lightheaded and dizzy. The world seemed to shift and spin.

But I needed to hold it together. Bending over, I braced my hands on my knees. Took slow breaths.

"Olivia."

I opened my eyes. Erik crouched in front of me, the spear at his side. His pale gaze searched my face.

"You're all right?" he asked softly.

Swallowing hard, I nodded. Despite that response, he remained there, watching me until I straightened up again. When he rose to his feet, the spear stood taller than his own considerable height.

Now he intended to use that weapon.

Heart racing, I looked through the portcullis. Orange streaked the darkening sky. The shadows between the trees had deepened and spread across the clearing. There was still enough light to see by, but night came quickly in the mountains. "Are you sure you'll be okay out there?"

"Yes." No hesitation.

"But he said you were weak."

"Not while I still have some control."

I glanced back at him. "Why wouldn't you have control? Is that the curse he was talking about? What does it do?"

Erik didn't answer. Jaw tight, he stepped inside the house to push up the lever. The portcullis rattled and began to rise. "You'll be safe in here. Lower this again as soon as I'm outside."

God. I looked out into the clearing again, and into the darkness of the trees beyond. Erik would be out there. Alone. "I have my gun. If you're not going to tell me what the curse is, at least tell me how I can help."

"You'll help by staying where I know you're safe," he said gruffly. "And when they're dead, by getting as far away from me as you can."

Because he couldn't stand to be near me. Because he might hurt me. Both were practical reasons to go. Both accounted for the aching knot in my throat.

So did knowing that I could do nothing to help him.

"All right." I nodded and turned blindly toward the house. "Good luck out there, then. And be careful."

For a man who couldn't wait to get rid of me, he wasn't in a hurry to go. When I faced him again, my hand on the portcullis lever, he still stood in the same spot, watching me. Within the shadows of the gatehouse, his eyes glowed with that feverish blue light and his features were starkly drawn, as if by pain—or hunger.

Frozen by that intense stare, I whispered, "Erik?"

It was as if I'd hit him. His head snapped around, tearing his gaze from mine. "*No,*" he bit out, and I didn't know if he was telling me or himself. But I didn't get a chance to ask.

Spear in hand, he strode out into the snow.

WHERE WAS HE? MY GAZE searched the shadows between the trees again. The moon had risen with the setting of the sun and silvery light flooded the clearing in front of the house. Everything beyond the clearing lay in darkness.

Almost an hour had passed without a sign of Erik, the Hounds, or the wolves. I'd gone into the house once, hoping to see something through the windows at the sides and rear of the fortress, but the narrow arrow slits on the first floor didn't offer much visibility, and the increasing clouds were reducing the visibility even more. Though the tower rooms had a more expansive view, I couldn't see any farther into the trees than I did from the gatehouse. So I'd returned outside and waited.

Now I was considering going back into the house and searching for some clue that could tell me what the hell was going on. I'd tried to look up "moon hound" on my phone and stared stupidly at a blank browser screen for a few seconds before remembering I didn't have service. One of the bedrooms upstairs had shelves stuffed full of books, though. I'd probably find something there. On the job, Erik fixed problems. If he was suffering from a curse, he'd have tried to fix that, too—which meant he must have researched it. Even if I couldn't quickly find a real answer, simply reading the titles might offer a hint.

But not yet. Movement at the edge of the clearing sent my heart leaping into my throat.

Erik. Though I couldn't see more than his silhouetted frame, his height and the breadth of his shoulders were unmistakable.

Except…he'd said the Hounds might disguise themselves. That one might trick me into seeing Erik in his place. It seemed crazy, but so did blue skin. My pulse racing, I tugged off my right glove and slipped my hand into my bag. The pistol grip was cold against my palm.

Before I could call out, his warning came across the clearing. "Don't raise the gate."

"I won't."

"Where's your gun?" He was closer now.

"I've got it here."

"You're going to need it, Olivia. So take it out."

Suddenly alarmed, I did. "Why?"

He reached the portcullis. The light spilling from the open front door revealed the bleak torment of his face. His hands wrapped around the bars like a man imprisoned, even though I was the one locked in. "Because you have to kill me."

My stomach lurched. Why would he say something like that? It had to be a joke...even though he looked deadly serious.

But I couldn't believe he meant it. "That's *really* not funny."

"I know." His hoarse agreement twisted the pain in my chest a little deeper. "But it's the only way. Inside the house, you'll be safe from the Hounds. You won't be safe from me."

"Why? What will you do?" Frustration boiled through me when he only shook his head. "Then how do I know this isn't a trick? That you're not a Hound, trying to...I don't know. *Trick* me."

Into killing him. That made even less sense than Erik asking me to shoot *him.*

"Ask me something only you would know."

I'd already thought of the question I would use to verify his identity. "That night we went over the plans at the D&G offices, we went out to dinner when we were done. Where did we go?"

"We didn't go out." His irises blazed a pale blue and his gaze fell to my lips. "We ordered in. Pizza."

I hadn't wanted him to be right. But this was Erik. And he was telling me to kill him.

There was no way. No fucking way.

As if my face revealed exactly what I was thinking, Erik rasped, "You *have* to do it."

"No." Pissed now, I stalked into the house.

"Don't you— God damn it, Olivia!"

The iron lever shrieked when I shoved it up, raising the gate. My gun still in hand, I stepped outside again as it rattled upward.

As soon as the spikes at the bottom cleared his chest, Erik ducked underneath and pushed past me. The lever screeched down. He joined me in the gate-house again, so big in the narrow space between the portcullis and the door. "You have to do it."

"Why? What will you do?"

"Nothing, if you listen to me. The Hounds are

still out there. Even after you shoot me, the house will still protect you from them." Calm acceptance had smoothed his expression, as if in his mind I'd agreed to kill him—and he was perfectly okay with that. "But you still have to be careful—"

"I'm *not* murdering you, Erik."

"—because they'll be pissed that I didn't wait for them to do it," Erik continued, talking right over me. "You have to shoot me between the eyes. Anywhere else will barely slow me down. Then leave my body out here. When the sheriff or someone else sees your Jeep on the road, they'll come up the drive to find out what happened. The Hounds won't risk exposing themselves then. So tell whoever comes that I attacked you—that I was the one who destroyed your rig. It'll be self defense."

He had it all planned out. Not just resigned to this fate, but determined for me to kill him. Why did he think I could?

Shaking my head, I dropped the gun into my bag. "This isn't happening."

His appearance of calm cracked. Blue eyes paled to diamond. His lips drew back in a terrifying grimace, revealing those sharpened teeth. Instinctively I backed up until my shoulders pressed against the granite blocks of the gatehouse wall.

He came after me. His palms slammed against stone on either side of my shoulders, caging me in. My insides quaking, I thought of the gun I'd just put in my bag. I wouldn't use it. But, oh God, I wished that I still had it in my hand. Instead I stood with my fingers clenched, my body shaking.

Looming over me, he bent his head to mine. "It *has* to happen, Olivia."

"Why? Explain to me why, Erik! And maybe I'll do it."

That was a lie. I couldn't. But if he would at least tell me what might happen, I could prepare for it.

"You heard what the Hound said. That I'll come through stone to get you. I will, Olivia. The curse doesn't let me kill myself to stop it, so you have to. I thought that if I was away from you, if I didn't know where you were, it would be all right. But I can *feel* you, like there's a chain pulling me toward you, and it's getting stronger. If you leave now, I'll track you down. There's nowhere to run. And when I find you, I'll force— I'll..." His voice faltered before hardening again. "I'll *hurt* you, Olivia. So you have to do this."

His gaze burned into mine, pleading, and I tried to imagine myself doing as he'd asked, of simply aiming the gun and pulling the trigger.

"I can't," I whispered. My heart constricted when his eyes closed and his head hung in defeat. "Not in cold blood. If you actually attack me, maybe. But not like this, not here—"

His head shot up, his eyes blazing and razored teeth bared. He lunged at my neck. I screamed and flinched to the side. My hand dove into my bag at the same moment I realized what he'd done. I changed course and swung.

My palm cracked across his cheek. "Don't you *dare* try to scare me into it now!"

Erik went rigid. Slowly, the corners of his mouth curved upward. "Olivia."

Just my name, but I heard the warmth in his tone. Great. He thought my response was commendable. As for me, I wondered if my refusal to shoot him was the stupidest choice I'd ever made.

But there had to be other options.

"Okay, look." I couldn't stop my voice from shaking in reaction and fear, but I was determined to approach this sensibly. "You said it was a curse. Can't curses be broken?"

"Yes," he said, then dashed my hope. "This curse on my family will break during Ragnarök, when Odin's son Víðarr destroys Loki's son, Fenrir the Wolf."

A weak laugh escaped me. I didn't know all of those names, but I knew some of them: Odin and Loki, both Norse gods…and Ragnarök. "During the end of the world?"

He nodded, his gaze holding mine.

Not a good option, then. "What about the curse itself? Someone had to cast it, right?"

"The Witch of the Ironwood."

"Can't she be reasoned with? Maybe someone in my mom's family—"

"She's been dead for a thousand years."

Shit. "That's inconvenient."

I bit my lip when a low laugh rumbled from him, suddenly aware that his arms still caged me in against the gatehouse wall. Despite the sharp teeth, the strange blue skin, and his enormous size, my fear of him was fading. Maybe that was stupid. But he was trying so hard to protect me, so willing to sacrifice his own life to avoid giving in to the curse, I couldn't believe that he'd hurt me.

Why would anyone force him to hurt me in the first place? "Why did she curse your family?"

"We are Víðarr's descendants," he said. "And the witch was both Fenrir's lover and mother to his son, the Moon Hound."

"And the brothers waiting to kill you are the

descendants of the Moon Hound?" That kind of made sense. "So she cursed your family in revenge, because Víðarr killed Fenrir. Or *will* kill Fenrir, during the apocalypse."

Which, as far as I knew, hadn't happened yet. And thinking about it further, now it didn't make any sense at all. I shook my head.

"Okay, wait. Why are they coming after you, then? None of that has happened yet."

"The eldest brothers don't have any more choice than I do—but some aren't compelled. They come to avenge the fallen ones. Our families just play out the same battle over and over again, and will until the final battle takes place."

The same battle? Erik had said that Víðarr won his. "Do the Hounds ever win?"

"On the winter solstice, they can." His answer stopped my heart. "When the curse is at its strongest. When we're weak."

"Weak…? Because you're overcome with the need to kill someone else?"

"Not kill, but—" His eyes closed again. "It's the same. We focus on getting to them. There's nothing else. So the Hounds can take advantage of our distraction."

"So basically some innocent person is sacrificed

so that a Hound has a chance of winning? That's an *awful* thing to curse someone with."

A bleak smile was his only response. Cold seeped through me as I pondered the implications of it. The curse wasn't just horrible for Erik, but for anyone caught near him…and the solstice came every year.

"How many?" I had to know. Maybe I *would* shoot him. "How many people have you hurt? How many have you killed?"

"None!" His expression darkened and a shudder ripped through him. Jaw clenching, he stilled his body again. "I swear to you, Olivia. None."

Confusion replaced my anger. "Then what makes this solstice different?"

"Some of us never fall under the curse. I didn't… until recently."

"Well, what changed? Can you change it back?"

"No." He shook his head and gave a humorless laugh. "No, I can't."

"But something *did* change. Right?"

"Yes." His gaze fell to my mouth. "I kissed you."

Shock silenced me. I couldn't breathe.

"I shouldn't have," he continued roughly. "Walking away might have saved us both…but maybe it wouldn't have mattered. Maybe it was all over the second I met you, because you'd still be the same woman whether I kissed you or not."

"But..." I'd had this all wrong. "You aren't coming after me because I'm near you? You're after *me* specifically?"

His answer was a slow nod.

What difference did it make who I was? I grasped for a reason—and found one that seemed to make sense. "Because I have a witch's blood?"

For a long second, he regarded me in silence. I wished that I could read his face, but his thoughts remained hidden behind diamond eyes and a faint smile.

"You have something, Olivia," he finally said. "What power do you wield, then?"

"None. I didn't inherit anything from her." Except for a deep practical streak and strong instincts that had already steered me in the wrong direction regarding Erik. "My mother says the abilities skip a generation. So my daughter will have it."

A fire lit behind his eyes. "And your sons?"

I shook my head. "We only have girls in my family."

"We only have boys." His smile widened when I laughed. "So this is why you're not terrified, faced with me now. You're no stranger to magic."

"A part of me is scared shitless," I admitted, then wished I hadn't when his smile vanished. "But you're right: it's easy for me to accept this craziness. It's not so easy to accept that you can't do anything to stop it."

"*You* can," he said softly.

By shooting him? "No. There has to be another option. You said this started when you kissed me. That was over a year ago. What were you doing during the last winter solstice?"

"My father was here with me. He shattered my bones with an axe so that I couldn't go after you. When I healed, he did it again."

I stared up at him in horror. "What?"

"He refused to do it this year." His jaw hardened. "I hoped that if I didn't know where you were, you'd be safe, even if I destroyed myself trying to find you. But he sent you straight to me."

Gulbrandr *had* sent me here. There was only one reason I could imagine him doing something like that. "So if I kill you, I'm safe, right? But what happens if you kill *me*? Will you still be affected by the curse?"

Erik's tormented silence was my answer. Oh, God. My breath hitched.

Suddenly fierce, he leaned in, his blue lips

pulled back from sharp teeth. "I *won't* hurt you. Because you're going to shoot me first."

Reeling, I could only shake my head. Accepting magic was one thing. Knowing that John Gulbrandr had forced us into this situation was another. He'd sacrificed me to help his son. No wonder Erik had said that he'd kill his father—I was feeling pretty murderous toward Gulbrandr, too. There was no chance that I would continue working for him, not after this.

This had turned out to be a really shitty detour. Now I had no job, and no way out of this.

So why hadn't my mother sent me running?

"What about your dad, Erik? What about your mom? He must have kissed her." I'd met her at the firm's Christmas party only a few days before. A pediatrician with a warm smile, she'd spent the evening at John Gulbrandr's side. I wouldn't have said they appeared to be the most affectionate or loving couple, but I hadn't noticed any tension between them. "She didn't look like a woman who feared what her husband would do to her within a week."

Erik seemed to still. His icy gaze held mine. "It wasn't the kiss. And my father has never been affected by the curse."

"Why? So is it the witch's blood?" When he shook his head, I pressed further. "Does the curse always target a woman?"

"Usually," he said roughly.

"And was your grandfather affected?"

"Yes."

"Who did he focus on?"

For a long second, I didn't think he would answer. Then he said, "My grandmother."

"Did he hurt her?"

"I don't know," Erik said. "She died before I was born."

Oh, Jesus. "Did your grandfather kill her?"

If he had, I was taking Erik's truck and getting the hell away from him. Screw the Hounds.

But even as I thought it, I remembered what they'd had done to my Jeep. Erik had a nice rig with four-wheel drive, but I didn't want to risk getting stuck in the driveway. I'd be a sitting duck. Better to stay at his fortress than ride away in a truck that the Hounds could rip apart. I'd rather take my chances with Erik, and pray that he could maintain control.

"No," he said. "My grandfather built this house to keep her safe from the Hounds on those nights. But a car wreck took her, instead."

An accidental death. Sad, but a relief for me to

hear now. "Did your grandfather ever talk about what happened?"

"About his time with her?" Erik shook his head. "Her death destroyed him. He never mentioned her without breaking down. So I never asked."

"How many years did he have with her?"

"Almost twenty."

"So she survived twenty solstices," I said pointedly.

His response emerged on a frustrated growl. "That doesn't change anything. *You* might not survive one."

"Well, what about everyone else in your family?" I knew he didn't have any siblings. "Aunts and uncles? Cousins? Are they cursed, too?"

"No."

So Erik had never actually seen or heard a first-hand account of what happened, and he didn't really know that hurting me was inevitable. That didn't surprise me. It was hard to believe that such brutality could continue unchecked for over a thousand years in one family. Someone would avenge the women or protect them—a mother or father, sisters or brothers. If Erik hurt me, my family would come down on him like the fury of Hell. In a thousand years, surely other families would have done the same? If the Gulbrandrs were so terrible, they should have been wiped off the face of the earth by now.

But they hadn't been. "There *has* to be some solution or my mother would have warned me away. So we'll find it."

"God, Olivia. You're so damned practical and determined. I never had a chance." His heavy sigh whispered across my cheek in a cold caress. "But practicality can't stop this curse. Neither can determination. Do you think that we haven't tried? For a thousand years, men stronger than me, smarter than me, braver than me. We all fell."

Perhaps, but the practical side of me couldn't give up. "You're resisting it now," I pointed out.

His diamond gaze locked on mine. "Barely."

My eyes widened. How could that be true? He didn't give a sign of it. When I'd first arrived, he'd seemed closer to the edge of control, shaking and feverish. Now he didn't appear to be in pain, but as solid as stone. Definitely not on the verge of—*oh, God*.

All this time, I hadn't looked away from his face. Now when I looked down, I was stunned to see the aggressive thrust of his cock behind denim, but his enormous arousal didn't astonish me as much as his feet did. From his knees to the ground, two thick columns of ice cemented his legs in place.

"Your feet," I gasped. "Did you do that to yourself?"

"Yes. The ice can't stop me. But it helps me maintain control."

Not just his legs, I realized. He'd fused his hands to the wall, too, surrounding me in a sculpture of flesh, ice, and stone.

This was crazy. "How close are you to losing it?"

"Close enough." His voice roughened and a shiver raced over my skin. "It will only become worse. The astronomical solstice is two nights away. From now until then, only a miracle or a bullet will keep me off of you. And you're a practical woman, Olivia. You know a bullet has a better chance."

God, that was true. But I wouldn't admit it. "Don't rule a miracle out," I said. "After all, it's almost Christmas."

A moment of silence fell between us, then a deep laugh rumbled from him. Erik shook his head, and as my own laugh burst into the frozen air between us, I realized that I couldn't see his breath. He stilled when my hand lifted to his lips.

"Olivia—"

"Hush." I interrupted his warning. "Just control

yourself."

"I *am*," he gritted out—then went silent, his eyes closed and teeth clenched as my fingers traced the strong line of his jaw. Rough, unshaven.

Burning.

But his breath had been cold—though there wasn't any at all now. "*Breathe*, Erik."

His frigid exhalation crossed my fingertips… even though I could still feel the heat radiating from his skin. Cursed with a fever, yet freezing inside.

Beside my shoulders, the ice climbed farther up his arms.

I was pushing his control too far. Reluctantly, I pulled my hand back. "Is this ice and cold inside you from the curse, too? Or is this you?"

"It's me." His glittering eyes met mine again. "Mostly a man. Some frost giant. That's the part I'm holding back."

Frost giant? I suppose that explained his size. Though not absurdly tall, he was a big man—and I'd always liked that about him. I'd liked his large hands and broad shoulders, and I'd always assumed that he'd be big all over.

Unless he had a giant icicle in his jeans, he *was* big all over. But I didn't let myself look down again. Touching him, having him so close was pushing my mind in a direction that it shouldn't be going—and an erection didn't mean anything. He was hard all over, so a hard dick didn't necessarily mean he wanted me. It might just be something else he couldn't control.

"So you're holding the frost giant back. But you don't *know* that you'll hurt me if you let it out? You just worry that you will because you're strong and you've never had this happen before." I knew it was a fine line to draw, but his life lay on that line and it was worth examining. "But your grandmother survived the curse, didn't she? So there's a chance you won't hurt me, and my choice is to take that risk or to kill you."

"Your only choice is to kill me."

I couldn't accept that. I *wouldn't* accept it.

He must have read that determination on my face. Shaking his head, he began roughly, "Olivia—"

"We'll think of a plan," I said. "Maybe I'll end up shooting you. Maybe I won't. But we have to *try*, all right?"

"No." He ground out the denial through clenched teeth. "It's too dangerous."

"Dangerous? Jesus Christ. What do you think shooting you in cold blood will do to me? Do you think it wouldn't completely fuck me up? Do you think the guilt wouldn't destroy me and that I wouldn't spend the rest of my life hating myself because I didn't try harder?" My voice broke as I imagined watching the life drain from his eyes, then imagined trying to get through the rest of the day. And the next. And the next. "How can I bear knowing that I murdered you? Nothing you've done justifies it."

Desolation swept across his features. "Not yet. But I will."

"How do you know? My mother *sees the future* and even that isn't inevitable. So I have to try. I have to. Now let's go inside and talk about it…while you still can."

Breathlessly, I waited for his answer. His gaze searched mine. He finally relented with a heavy sigh.

"Go in, then."

Chapter Four

Despite agreeing to try, Erik didn't immediately follow me into the house. One look back at him told me why. Shattered ice lay in heaps near his feet. It no longer encased his arms and legs, no longer helped him maintain control—and the effort showed. He stood with his head down and his hands braced against the gatehouse wall. The tendons in his neck stood out in stark relief against his blue skin, every muscle in his body straining.

Watching him, I couldn't mistake the power of that curse. Despite his strength of will, Erik believed it would overpower him; I believed it now, too. But watching him told me more: how hard he'd fight to keep from hurting me when it did.

I had to trust in that. The only other choice would destroy us both. "Erik?"

As if in response to my voice, a shudder ripped through his big body and he rasped, "I need a minute, Olivia."

To regain control. That would probably be easier if I was out of his sight, and a minute alone would do me good, too. I'd barely had a second to think since I'd seen the claw marks on my Jeep. I needed to put my thoughts in order and calm the chaotic emotions roiling inside me—and hopefully come up with a plan that would leave us both alive.

I had no idea what that plan would be.

Troubled, I ventured from the foyer into the great room, shrugging out of my coat and stripping off my hat. I left my vest on. Though not cold enough to see my breath, the house was chilly. Luckily, wood had been stacked near the fireplace and kindling lay ready in the grate.

Sinking to my heels in front of the firebox, I fished a lighter from my bag, then recalled Erik's fever when I'd first arrived. He'd been affected by the curse before he'd even seen me—and he'd probably kept the house cold on purpose. Compared to what he was going through, I could stand a little chill.

I replaced the lighter and glanced up. A walnut beam served as a mantel shelf. Over it, the iron brackets that held Erik's spear stood empty. Soon Erik would use that weapon. He'd either kill the brothers in the woods or be killed—and the Hounds believed that whatever Erik did to me on the solstice would make him welcome death.

I couldn't bear to let him die. So how was I going to stop it?

A sofa faced the fireplace. Stripping off my gloves, I sank onto a cushion and pushed my fingers into my hair. My brain seemed to work best in this position. But my thoughts weren't leading toward a solution—only more heartache and dread.

The Hounds were wrong. Erik wouldn't wait until the solstice; he already sought death. Despite his wish, I couldn't help him find it. He hadn't hurt me yet, and—

My brain ground to a halt. Painful emotion tore at my chest as realization hit me.

Erik *had* hurt me. While walking with me to my Jeep, he'd eviscerated me with words. But he shouldn't have been able to. Not that deeply.

Unless I felt more for him than I'd been willing to admit.

His declaration rang through my mind again. *I*

left to get away from you, Olivia. I can't stand being around you. The memory formed a hollow echo inside my guts, the insistent ache of a wound that might never heal—but it shouldn't have felt any worse than a slap. I'd been rejected by men before. It always stung; then I got over it.

I didn't think I'd get over this. For a year and a half, I'd told myself that I was only attracted to him. But I couldn't fool myself anymore—Erik had only been able to rip out part of my heart because I felt more than simple attraction.

"Olivia?"

I jerked my head up. Erik stood at the door, looking like himself again. No blue skin or claws. Just big and gorgeous and his intense gaze locked on mine. My stomach clenched at the sight of him, but instead of resenting it, I wondered how I'd never recognized what that reaction meant. Not just attraction, but excitement and hope that I'd always hastily quashed.

I didn't suppress it now. And I couldn't imagine the effort it had taken for him to rein in the curse and the frost giant within, but I could see it. His eyes burned feverishly blue again and his entire body had stiffened, as if warding away pain.

My gaze returned to his face. "How long? You'll

be okay until the solstice, right?"

"I don't know. It might hit me in an hour. It might take another day."

"When did it hit last year?"

"The night of the solstice. But you weren't this close to me then. It's already worse. To be safe, you need to do it soon."

Kill him? Stricken, I shook my head. "You can't ask this of me."

"It's too much to ask of anyone." His voice sounded as if sandpaper lined his throat. "But you have to do it."

Shoot him? Resolve firmed my response. "I can't. Not when you haven't done anything to me yet. Not when a curse is forcing you to do it."

"That's bullshit. You can't blame a rabid dog for his disease, but you'd still put him down before he bites someone."

"You're not a dog, Erik."

"But I'm not completely human, either." His head lifted. Blue tinged his skin again. "You're a practical woman. You *can* do this."

I gave a wild laugh, shaking my head. No, I wasn't practical. I couldn't be in regards to him.

His tone hardened. "Do you think nothing will happen because your mother didn't warn you? You don't have phone reception here. How do you know she hasn't left another message telling you to run for your life?"

I couldn't know. But my mother wasn't the only reason why I didn't think he'd hurt me. His insistence that I kill him said he'd shield me from harm instead.

"We'll work out a fix," I said. "So just help me out, okay?"

Though his jaw tightened again as if he wanted to argue, Erik gave a small nod.

"We've got two problems: the Hounds and the curse. But we've got two days. So as long as you keep control until the night of the— No, shut up." I stopped him when I saw that he was going to interrupt. "You *are* going to keep control until then. You don't have another choice."

I don't know if Erik nodded again just to placate me or if he really believed he could. It didn't matter. He would do it.

"All right," I continued. "Problem one are the Hounds. I'm safe from them in here, right?"

"Right."

"But I'm not safe from you. So even though you don't know for certain that you'll hurt me, there's zero chance that I'll reach Day Three without *some-*

thing happening."

His voice roughened. "Right. Unless you shoot me."

"Don't start that again," I warned him.

He held my gaze—no backing down.

So frost giants were stubborn assholes. Fine. I was stubborn, too. "If I'll be safe here, then what if you go? If you leave right now and just go as far as you can? If you keep control until the night of the twenty-first, and only lose it for a few hours, maybe you'll come to your senses again before you make it back. "

Erik was already shaking his head. "I wouldn't get far. The curse will pull me back to you. And if I lose control when I'm out there, I'll come through these walls—giving the Hounds a way in."

That would suck for us both. "So the first priority has to be getting rid of the Hounds. Because I'll be okay here tonight, maybe even tomorrow night, but by the night of the twenty-first I need to be gone."

"That's too late. It won't matter by then—you can't get far enough."

Come on. "Even if I drive out of here? You're faster than your truck?"

"Yes."

Shit. "I guess that might not be an option

anyway. There's going to be a lot more snow coming down soon and we can't call a plow."

"A plow doesn't matter," he said. "I can clear the driveway."

Remembering how he'd skimmed over the snow earlier, something told me that he wouldn't be clearing it with a snowblower or a shovel. "How far do I need to be?"

"Australia." He didn't sound as if he was kidding. "A flight?"

Erik was quiet for a long moment, and this time when he nodded, I didn't think it was just to placate me. Instead a bit of hope had lightened the bleak resignation clouding his face.

"So frost giants can't fly," I said.

A quick smile broke through. "No."

That was the answer, then. I just had to—*oh, shit*. It was the freaking holidays. And international travel might be out if the only open flights went somewhere that required getting a visa in advance. "What if I only make it to Houston or New York? Is that far enough? What if I just hop around the country?"

Though that wouldn't be easy, either. Not with the weather and holiday travel mucking up every-thing. Plus, the snowstorm rolling in over Denver might shut down the airport entirely.

The hope seeping from his expression told me the answer. "You have to land. And if there were delays—"

"Okay," I said, nixing that idea. No way would a dead end stop me, though. I'd turn around and try again. "If there's zero chance of getting to Day Three here, then even a one-percent chance somewhere else is better. So what happens if I drive out of here now? Maybe I'll get far enough. Maybe you won't find me. So is that an option? The Hounds are here for you, not for me. Would they let me go through?"

His eyes paled to diamond. "No. They've already destroyed your Jeep. They're here for revenge and they'll use you to get to me."

Yeah, that was what I figured. The brothers would wreck the truck, capture me, and both Erik and I would be in a worse position than we were now.

"But I could go with you," Erik continued slowly. "Draw them out. When they come after us, when they reveal themselves, I stop them—and you keep driving."

That idea started out better than it finished. "Drive on while you're fighting? Just leave you?"

"Yes."

"What if—"

"You drive on."

God damn it. "But what if—"

"No!" The sudden snap of sharpened teeth made my heart jump. His fists clenched in his jeans and he stared at me, eyes blazing blue again. "There are two possible outcomes. One is that I win—then you need to get away from me. One is that I lose—then you need to get away from the Hounds. Either way, *you keep driving.*"

"Three!" I snapped back. "*Three* possible outcomes. And the third is that while you're fighting the others, one of the brothers comes after me anyway. Are you sure you can take all three Hounds at once without losing one?"

He wasn't sure. I could see it in the way he suddenly ripped his hands through his hair in frustration, but also in the way he didn't respond. He was quiet, his jaw tight—reconsidering our options.

"I'll have to kill at least one of them first," he finally said. Determination hardened his gaze. "But better if I take out two before we try to go. Tonight and tomorrow, I'll hunt them down. Then you'll take my truck. If any Hounds are left, we'll draw them out."

All right. Though far from a perfect plan, at least it was better.

"But if I can't hold out," he added softly, "if I come after you, you have to shoot me in the head. Anywhere else won't matter. I'll show you."

ERIK CONTINUED INTO THE KITCHEN. Wary—wondering exactly *how* he would show me—I followed him. Like the great room, the kitchen appeared deceptively bright and warm, considering how few windows allowed in the light. It was also just as big, flowing past a rustic seating area and into an open, formal dining room that lay near the front of the house.

As if recognizing the presence of food, my stomach rumbled. I ignored it. Eating wasn't high on my list of priorities right now.

Erik pulled a knife from a block on the center island. After a glance my way, he laid his left hand flat on the cutting board.

This was what he meant to show me? My heart thumped wildly. "You are *not*."

"I am," he said. "I don't want you to think that you can just shoot the Hounds—or me—anywhere but the head and still expect to stop us."

"But—"

He stabbed the back of his hand. I slapped my palms over my mouth, stopping my scream—then muffling my gasp, because the blade had slid off as if his skin were made of steel.

"This is why I can't jump off a cliff and stop the curse," he said softly. "I could shoot myself with your gun and it wouldn't do anything. Try it."

"Shoot you?"

"Later." Smiling a little, he held out the knife. "Go on."

"I don't think so." But I was curious. "Let me see you stab it again."

He did, but not his hand. My whole body flinched when he aimed the knife toward his heart—but the blade only ripped through the gray t-shirt, exposing a slice of skin beneath. No blood. Not even a scrape.

Just a hard pectoral muscle dusted with dark hair. At least I had an excuse to stare.

He held out the knife again. Dubious, I glanced at it. "I won't hurt you?"

"No."

"Then what good is shooting you?" Or the Hounds.

"It's an exception. Nothing else can kill me."

That was a good thing. But also crazy. "How do you even learn something like that? What did the men in your family do—sit around shooting each other until you figured that out?"

"Close enough."

That wasn't the answer I expected. With a laugh, I asked, "Seriously?"

A quick grin touched his mouth. "Invulnerability made some of them reckless. My grandfather told me how one of his great-uncles used to go around to taverns, making wagers that he could survive a musket shot to the chest. After a while, no one would take the bet anymore—so he upped the stakes and wagered that he could survive a shot to the head. He lost, and we figured out that as long as we're not pulling the trigger, a bullet in the brain would kill us."

"Oh, God." I shouldn't laugh. But I was. And Erik was smiling, too, so he must not have taken offense on behalf of his uncle.

He slid the knife toward me. "Try it."

I came closer, setting my bag on one of the barstools tucked up to the island. The knife handle was still heated by his grip. Erik flattened his hand against the counter, pale blue skin over gleaming black granite. I glanced up at him and he nodded.

I couldn't believe I was doing this. But I wasn't just going to *stab* him. I wanted to see how that steel-skin thing worked.

It didn't. I dragged the point of the knife over the back of his hand. A line of blood welled up behind it.

"Oh, my God!" The knife clattered to the counter and I scrambled for the roll of paper towels standing beside the sink. "I'm sorry. I'm so sorry."

He tried to stop me. "Olivia, it's all right."

No, it wasn't. Throat tight, I pressed the wad of paper to the back of his hand. "Goddammit. Why didn't that work? The witch's blood again?"

"No." His uninjured hand covered mine. "It's all right. Look."

Something inside me stilled. I looked up and saw the faint amusement in his smile. "You *knew* I'd be able to do that?"

"Yes. I needed to show you—"

"Because *telling* me wouldn't accomplish the same thing?" I jerked my hands out from under his. My eyes were stinging. Jesus. I could have stabbed him. Maybe even right through the heart. I might have *killed* him. "You really felt you had to trick me into it?"

Amusement gone, his face darkened. "No."

But he had. He'd said I couldn't hurt him. And I'd been stupid enough to fall for it. Because now I remembered how slamming my foot between his legs had dropped him to his knees.

If he hadn't been on the other side of the island, I might have given him another swift kick. Instead I turned and walked away, my vision a blur and my throat a solid knot. I didn't know where I was going. Back to the great room, maybe. Anywhere to be away from the stupid jackass who apparently thought that I could cut into someone and think it was all a joke.

"Olivia."

My name sounded like the crack of a glacier— and came from directly behind me. It was all the warning I got. A steel band snagged around my waist and spun me to face him. My chest hit a solid wall of muscle. Wildly I fought for leverage, shoving against him, but he didn't give an inch. His fingers tightened in my hair, forcing my head back. Frigid breath skimmed the side of my neck.

Sudden terror snagged me in a frozen grip as I remembered his sharp teeth. Would he bite me now? Rip my throat out?

God, I should have listened to him. I should have shot him.

"Erik?" Fear made my voice sharp. Could he even hear me? "Erik, you're losing it. You need to get this under—"

Burning heat suddenly swept up my throat, followed by shocking cold. An involuntary shiver tightened my skin—then stunned disbelief stole my breath as I realized what he'd done.

Erik had licked me.

Licked me.

Then groaned in pleasure, a sound so raw and carnal that my fear melted away in the rush of heat. That groan told me Erik was ravenous, but not for a bite. Just for a taste.

I shuddered as he tasted me again, his fevered lips hot and his mouth cold. His tongue slicked from the hollow of my throat to the edge of my jaw, drawing another tremor from my tense muscles. Though my heart thundered, I couldn't move, couldn't speak. This wasn't what I'd expected, and no matter how many times I'd dreamed of this, my brain hadn't yet caught up with the response of my body. I simply couldn't believe that Erik was holding me and burning the length of my throat with his lips.

Even though he couldn't stand being around me.

A heavy knot lodged in my chest. No wonder my brain couldn't accept what was happening; some part of me must have recognized that it made no sense at all. He'd lost control and come after me. But he couldn't stand being near me, so this wasn't what he *wanted* to do. It was what the curse was *making* him do.

Hoarsely I said, "Put me down."

Erik growled. Abruptly the arm around my waist lifted me higher, dragging me up over the thick ridge of his erection. Uncontrollable need speared through me, a clenching ache between my thighs—but this *wasn't* going to happen right now. Not while my heart was hurting like this.

"Put me down, damn it!"

This time, my command must have gotten through to him. He stilled, but he didn't release me. He held me against his broad chest, his face buried in my throat, his breath cold and harsh against my neck.

I struggled against his grip. "Erik—"

"I can't let you go. God, Olivia." Agonized tension roughened his voice. "Do it now."

Shoot him? "I don't have my bag. So either get yourself under control *right now* or you're going to hurt me."

His big body stiffened. "I won't hurt you."

I knew he wouldn't intend to. But if he continued like this, he would. "Then *fight* it," I told him.

A shudder wracked his body. His head lifted. Ice began to climb his legs—but not his hands. "I can't let you go yet," he said hoarsely against my ear.

Just like before, when he'd taken a few minutes to regain control—except this time he was holding me. I nodded, trying to ignore the feel of his cock wedged into the juncture of my thighs, afraid the only sound that might emerge would be a needy whimper. He'd begun rocking between my legs—the barest of movements. I didn't even know if he was aware of doing it.

Breathlessly I said, "Tell me what happened. You had control just a few seconds ago."

"You walked away." His arm constricted around me. "And I lost it."

Okay. That made sense. The curse forced him to find me wherever I was. When it seemed like I was running away, the need to go after me over-whelmed him.

But I couldn't answer. The subtle movement between my thighs was slowly winding me up, and every time I tried to focus on something else another rock of his hips dragged my attention back to the increasing ache inside me, the wet and heat. God, I was on the verge of grinding against his rigid length just to ease the tension.

"I'm sorry, Olivia," he said softly. "The knife wasn't a trick."

Anger helped me find my voice again. "Then what the hell made you think that I'd want to hurt you any more than you like hurting me?"

"It didn't hurt me. That's what I wanted to show you. Look at my hand."

"I can't," I said tightly. "It's in my hair."

He froze, as if suddenly realizing exactly how he was holding me—his hips between my thighs, his fingers still fisted in the hair at my nape, his arm wrapped around my waist. In the silence I could almost hear my heart hammering against my ribs.

He'd held me like this before. I couldn't stop the memory sweeping through me, the sweet tension drawing each second out into an eternity that had begun eighteen months ago. I remembered the brush of his thumb, wiping away pizza sauce from the corner of my lips. The intensity of his pale blue gaze as it rose from my mouth to meet my eyes. The way he'd watched me as he'd leaned in, and the softness as our lips had met, his breath warming my skin. Then the hunger that pushed us to our feet and the sudden desperation in our kiss.

I could still hear his groan when my fingers had tangled in his hair and my mouth had opened beneath his. I could still taste him, the demanding thrust of his tongue, the slick heat. I could still feel his hand against my back, hauling me closer, and my absolute certainty that this man would be everything I'd wanted in a lover and partner and friend—and how he'd kissed me as if he never wanted it to end.

Yet it had ended. So quickly. In the months that had followed, I'd relived that kiss a thousand times, burning with hope and anticipation, still so certain that Erik would be mine. But even after I made the decision to forget him, I'd relived that kiss a thousand times more.

I imagined lifting my mouth to his now, to see if it would be anything like I remembered. But kissing him might destroy his control—and I wouldn't know if he kissed me because he wanted to, or because the curse didn't give him any other choice.

And he still hadn't let me go.

I thought he was trying to. He angled his head back, as if pulling away, but he didn't go far. He stopped with his mouth against my cheekbone, the stubble on his jaw gently scraping the delicate skin.

Another second passed, and I felt his silent struggle before the steel band of his arm finally loosened around my middle and his fingers eased from my hair. Releasing me.

I tried not to be sorry that he could. This was what I wanted—and I was supposed to be looking at his hand.

Mindful of the ice on the floor and the columns surrounding his feet and legs, I carefully turned—not breaking away, not running away. Just slowly pivoting and slipping out of his embrace, but still touching him. My fingers ran down his left forearm and he lifted his hand for my inspection.

No blood, no trace of the cut I'd made. Astonished, I skimmed the tip of my forefinger down the line that should have been there. Not even a scar. Just feverishly hot skin and strong fingers, the tendons in the back of his hand rigid beneath my touch.

"How quickly did it heal?"

"A few seconds."

The tautness of his reply made me look up. His eyes had paled again.

Maybe because I was all but stroking his hand.

I let him go, still standing close—still not running away. "So what did this have to do with the Hounds?"

His fingers clenched into a fist. Ice began climbing his arm. "I needed you to see that even though it *looks* like you're hurting us, you aren't."

"That's not true. I hurt you when I kicked you. You felt pain."

"For a few seconds. Not long enough. So a head shot is the only way. The blood doesn't mean anything—but the Hounds might have tricked you into believing it did."

I supposed that was true—and despite Erik telling me that I had to go for the head, if one of the Hounds had threatened me I *would* have shot his leg first. Or aimed for his chest, just because it was a bigger target. But unloading a full clip into a Hound would have hardly slowed him down.

A few seconds of pain. Oh, my God.

My heart in my throat, I whispered, "Last year, your dad used an axe to stop you from coming after me. Did it take any longer to heal than this cut did?"

His expression like a stone wall, Erik met my eyes. "No."

"Then he did it again?"

"Yes."

"*All night?*" Hundreds of times. Maybe thousands.

He answered with a short nod.

"Jesus, Erik." I didn't know what else to say. A few seconds to heal, then his bones shattered again. He couldn't tell me *that* hadn't hurt—or that over the course of the night, those few seconds hadn't added up to an agonizing hell. "No wonder he wouldn't do it again."

Erik's jaw clenched. Still pissed at his father for sending me here. So was I. But I couldn't blame the man for refusing to torture his son again.

And his son had withstood that torture to save me.

How could I ever repay him? Not with a bullet. "Erik—"

"Don't." Voice harsh, he shook his head. A thundercloud of a frown darkened his face. "Don't thank me for not hunting you down. Stopping himself is what a man *should* do, no matter what it takes. No gratitude necessary."

He was right. But not everyone took the hard road. Some people used any excuse possible *not* to take that road, and they were fully human, not laboring under a curse. So Erik had my gratitude whether he wanted it or not—and I would damn well discover a way to keep him from sacrificing himself for me again.

A sharp stone seemed lodged in my throat. After the way he'd come for me, I suspected that what he was sacrificing himself *for* wasn't exactly what he'd told me.

"When you attack me," I said slowly, "you're not going to try to kill me, are you? That's not what the curse is."

His jaw tightened. "Olivia—"

"I deserve to know, Erik."

But I already knew. The sudden despair that lined his face told me the truth.

Yet it was still a shock when Erik said hoarsely, "I'll fuck you." His rough response stole my breath, stopped every thought. "I won't have a choice. You won't either, because I'll come after you. I'll hold you down and force myself inside you. You can fight back, but I won't feel it. You can run, but I'll take you wherever I find you, even if you'll freeze to death in the snow. Even if you consented, I won't make you ready for me, and I won't stop until I'm done. So you have to stop me first."

By killing him. Because he might hurt me. But in the end, there wasn't much difference between what I thought before and what I knew now.

"Olivia," he said softly, and I knew that he was

going to tell me to shoot him again, but I couldn't bear to hear it.

Numbly I shook my head. "It changes nothing. Not really. Driving out of here is still my best option."

Teeth clenched and eyes diamond, he stared at my face for an endless moment before turning sharply away. His skin lightened to blue as he stalked into the hall. "I've got Hounds to kill. Then we'll get you the hell away from me."

CHAPTER FIVE

THE SNOW ARRIVED JUST AFTER TEN. FRIGID BLASTS of wind quickly followed. The temperature dropped. I held out as long as I could in the gatehouse. I might have lasted longer if I'd been moving around, but even using my hand warmers it was too cold to simply stand outside. The icy air seemed to be biting through my jeans as I searched for any sign of Erik in the swirling white. I hated leaving him out there alone with the Hounds—but I couldn't do anything to help, anyway, except to listen for his return and raise the portcullis again.

Inside the great room, I dragged off my boots and coat. Building a fire seemed like too much effort, so I simply curled up on the sofa and draped a heavy throw over my shivering body. While I warmed up, I forced myself to eat a protein bar from my bag, but only got halfway through it. The dense chocolate was hardened by the chill in the house, tough to chew, and sat like lead in my gut. Erik probably wouldn't care if I raided his kitchen for something better, but I didn't feel hungry anyway.

I hadn't felt much of anything since realizing what the curse was.

Even huddled beneath the thick blanket, I was numb all the way through. Hours had passed since Erik had told me the truth. The knowledge seemed wedged into my brain like the blade of an axe in a chunk of wood—so sharp and cold that I could barely think of anything else. But although I'd been constantly aware of the truth, I hadn't thought *beyond* it. I needed to, though, because the solstice wasn't that far away.

It changes nothing, I'd told him. That was mostly true. Erik still needed to stop the Hounds. I still needed to get away from him before he lost control.

But if I didn't get away, it changed everything. Because Erik fucking me was much different from him hurting me. One was terrifying, and I'd do anything to stop it.

One was something I wanted, and I'd probably

let it happen.

My throat burned. And there it was—the reason why I really didn't want to think about this. More than once in the past few hours, I'd caught myself imagining it…and my reaction hadn't been fear, but—God help me—excitement. *Arousal.* I hated myself for it. Under any other circumstances, my desire would have made sense. I'd fantasized about him for more than a year. But it didn't make sense now. We were in a horrifying situation. I should have been fighting it as hard as Erik was, yet I'd jumped straight to acceptance and was already planning to drop my panties.

Wrapping my mind around *that* seemed impossible. Was I so desperate to be with him? Or was I just desperate to feel as if I had some choice in the matter?

I didn't know. But now that I'd begun thinking, my brain wouldn't stop—and every thought only hurt more.

Erik had wanted to get away from me. Obviously the curse was to blame. He'd left the firm to protect me, but the warmth of that knowledge didn't last, because on its heels came another realization: the curse might be the only reason he'd wanted me in the first place. It might be the only reason he'd kissed me.

Maybe Erik hadn't left the firm just to stop himself from hurting me. Maybe he'd left because he couldn't stand how the curse made him need me.

If that was true, then he might not be asking me to kill him just to prevent his losing control and possibly hurting me; he also might be asking so that he wasn't forced to be with someone he didn't want.

God. I curled up tighter beneath the blanket, a thick ache building in my throat.

I didn't know what to do. If our situations were reversed, I couldn't swear that I wouldn't make the same choice that Erik had made. Maybe I'd rather be dead than hurt someone…or to have all of my choices taken away and be forced to fuck them. Maybe I should honor his decision.

But I couldn't shoot him. I couldn't.

And I could barely breathe, thinking that kiss so long ago—the incredible, soul-searing kiss that made my instincts scream that I'd found the love of my life—had been provoked by the curse instead of Erik wanting me.

So I didn't want to think anymore. My heart had taken too much of a beating today and every new realization was another blow. Exhaustion crept through me from bones to brain. Staring into the cold, dark fireplace, I let sleep come.

And hoped that I wouldn't think when I dreamed.

A TERRIFIED SCREAM IN MY ear ripped me from sleep. Heart pounding, I jolted up from the sofa and searched the darkened room.

No one was near.

Had I been dreaming? A nightmare? Cold sweat slicked my skin, but I didn't know if it was in reaction to my fear now or if I'd been terrified even while I'd slept. Maybe I'd woken myself with my own scream. The voice had sounded like a woman's.

It *was* a woman's. Every muscle in my body tensed as another shriek pierced the silence, coming from right behind me. Teeth chattering, I whipped around. No one here.

Was I going crazy?

"Erik!"

My voice, I realized in sudden horror. That was my voice...and the Hounds were tricksters.

"Oh my God. The Hounds are inside the house." Another bone-chilling scream was followed by a desperate shout. *"Erik, help me!"*

Oh, no. I raced for the door. An icy gust shoved

at the heavy wood and blasted my face. The fortress's thick stone walls had muffled the rising howl of the wind—not just a snowstorm now, but a raging blizzard. The light in the gatehouse ceiling barely penetrated the driving snow beyond the portcullis.

No sign of Erik. But it wouldn't be long.

"It's a trap, Erik!" I prayed my shout wasn't lost in the roar of the wind. "The Hounds aren't in here!"

They were probably waiting nearby, intending to attack as soon as he arrived.

Another scream came from behind me, rising higher and higher, as if I were suffering unimaginable torture. Even knowing it was fake, I was shaking by the time the scream abruptly stopped, my entire body stiff with terror.

A tall form suddenly emerged from the white. I stumbled back, muffling a shriek. It was Erik. Just Erik. His diamond eyes were wild, his face pale blue. His strong hands wrapped around the bars. "Olivia?"

Relief weakened my knees. I clung to the door frame to keep myself steady. "I'm all right. It was a trick. Maybe a trap for you."

"A trap." With narrowed eyes, he turned to study the snow behind him, the wind ripping the steam of his breath away. "All three coming for me."

"Yes—"

Another terrifying scream pierced the din of the storm. Erik spun to grip the portcullis bars again, his teeth sharp and his voice a rough growl. "Was that from *inside* the house?"

Unease squirreled down my spine. He'd been certain the Hounds couldn't get through the walls. But had they? Suddenly afraid of the darkness filling the room behind me, I whispered, "I don't know. But it sounds like it is."

"Jesus Christ." His knuckles whitened on the bars. "Let me in, Olivia. Hurry."

God, yes. I scrambled through the door and reached for the lever...then hesitated and looked back at Erik.

My mother insists that my strong instincts aren't magic. They aren't like an animal's instincts either, the innate force that sends birds flying south and baby turtles crawling into the sea. Instead she says that I notice things I'm not always consciously aware of, so my subconscious prods me in one direction or another. That's not unique; everybody's brain does it. My subconscious just prods a bit harder than most people's—and at that moment my instincts were like a sharp stick jabbing into my gut and warning me that something was horribly wrong.

Such as Erik asking me to raise the gate without first telling me to verify who he was. Maybe the urgency of the situation had made him forget, but now that I was trying to figure out exactly what had tripped my instincts, I began seeing more. His gray t-shirt should have been ripped across his chest from when he'd stabbed himself before. And I saw his breath, as if he was as warm on the inside as I was.

Not a frost giant. A Hound.

So this *had* been a trap, but not just for Erik. Instead the Hound had terrified me, hoping that I'd be so panicked that I'd forget to question him before raising the portcullis.

My hand dropped away from the lever. The Hound stared at my face for a long second, his jaw working. Slowly an abashed smile widened his mouth.

That wasn't Erik's smile.

"Damn," he said softly, and all at once his face changed in a liquid rearrangement of features, as if a new man had been poured beneath Erik's skin and seeped through his pores. Dark hair faded to silver—but unless this face was another mask, he wasn't the same Hound I'd seen in the woods before. One of the brothers, maybe. His hair was shorter, his features younger. Still wearing a t-shirt and jeans, he didn't seem so urbane or so predatory, just chagrined.

"So you found me out." Rueful amusement briefly danced in his yellow eyes, then his abashed grin faded into concern. "Okay, but listen. I'll admit to fooling you. But it's only because I've got to get you away from here."

"Right. Sure," I said pleasantly. "Fuck off."

"Do you know what he'll do to you? God." As if agitated, he pushed his hand through his hair. "*Yes,* I came here with my brothers to kill him. But we didn't know you'd be here. My brothers don't care, not really. I do. So I'll get you out of here. Now, while the storm can cover our escape."

Oh, he was good. Every expression, every gesture was a persuasive one. Too bad his actions didn't match his words.

"Then why trick me?" I asked. "You knew the screams might bring Erik here. Why not just knock softly so that we could sneak away?"

The Hound grinned again. "I can't really help that. The tricks are in my nature—in my blood. I couldn't pass up the opportunity. And if I kill him, you're out of danger, right?" His smile hardened. "Do you know what's in a frost giant's blood? Ice.

And he won't feel a thing when he rips you apart."

Rips me apart. I barely suppressed my shiver. I suspected that letting this man see how his words affected me would be like placing a weapon in his hands.

Maybe I'd already given too much away.

"Did you ask him why *you* are the one who triggered the curse?" His wolfish gaze had fixed on my face. "We heard what he said on the road—that he can't stand to be around you. That's the curse; that's why it's so terrible. It makes him need someone that he hates."

That had to be a lie. Erik didn't hate me. He might resent the curse, but he didn't hate me.

Still, my chest ached. I said hoarsely, "Then why is he protecting me?"

"Because he's not a monster," the Hound replied softly, but his piercing yellow eyes were still hard. "Not yet. On the solstice, he will be. And not many people can survive an angry fuck from a giant."

His grandmother had. For twenty years. Would she have remained that long with someone who hated her? Who repeatedly hurt her?

God, I didn't know. People often made decisions that I never would, but that made perfect sense to them. Maybe she'd chosen to stay...or maybe she had no other choice. Fifty years ago, a woman who slept with a man—because of a curse or not—probably risked more than I did. Maybe a frost giant seemed like a better deal than being a single mother or shunned by friends and family. Maybe she'd felt her only option had been staying.

But I couldn't think of this now—and I shouldn't believe a word this asshole was saying. Not when hurt and doubts could twist my instincts, making me vulnerable. That was probably what he wanted, so that I'd raise the gate and let him save me from Erik's brutality.

If it came to brutality, however, then I'd keep it between Erik and me. And I'd damn well save myself.

Stepping back, I gripped the edge of the door, preparing to close it in the Hound's face. He wasn't looking at me anymore, though. His body had stiffened and his nostrils flared as he scented the rushing wind.

The grin that widened his mouth then wasn't chagrined but horrifying, all glistening fangs and elongating jaw. Instead of pouring through his skin, this time the change ripped through him in an instant. I had only a glimpse of pointed ears, thick fur, and claws before he charged into the swirling snow.

Oh, shit. "Erik!" I screamed. "Erik, he's coming!"

The howling wind answered me. I couldn't see anything. Every noise seemed muffled by the storm. Was that a growl? A yelp?

A bundle of fur slammed into the iron bars and dropped to the ground. I screamed, reeling back. A giant figure strode into the faint light just as the Hound leapt to its feet, snarling.

The air suddenly seemed to tighten. With a rumble like rolling thunder, a thick sheet of white ice climbed the portcullis, creating a solid wall. The noise of the wind quieted.

Stunned, I stared at the ice sheet. Erik had done that, I realized. Making sure that I wasn't accidentally hurt while the battle raged outside.

He'd already hurt the Hound. Frozen blood glittered like rubies against the drifts of snow piled on the gatehouse floor. But even though the Hound had hit the bars hard enough to break bone and splatter blood, he'd been up again within seconds. To kill him, Erik would have to do far worse.

Perhaps he was protecting me from that, too. I didn't know which would be more frightening—seeing them fight, or not knowing what was happening. Because not knowing was pretty fucking terrifying. I kept thinking that I'd go inside for my gun and my boots, but I couldn't tear my gaze away from the sheet of ice. Once, something thudded against it so hard that the gatehouse shuddered—but the ice didn't crack. Then all was quiet again except for the pounding of my heart.

Even that seemed to stop as the ice shattered, collapsing into a pile at the base of the gate. Horror clutched my throat. Looking human except for his blue skin, Erik stood on the other side, clutching his spear—and covered in blood. His shirt had been shredded.

"Oh, my God." I had sense enough not to rush forward, but I had to grip the door frame to stop myself. "Are you all right?"

"Most of it isn't my blood." His voice was rough. His diamond gaze searched my face. "You?"

On the verge of bawling. But I didn't want to tell him. "That depends on whether you know what kind of statue Thomas Robertson wanted us to put in front of his building."

"A wookie," Erik said, and when my relieved laugh filled the gatehouse, he smiled.

That was the right smile. "Are you coming in?"

"I wouldn't mind changing out of these clothes." His gaze held mine. "But only if I won't scare you."

Because he was covered in blood. Because he'd just killed a Hound. But it wasn't Erik that I was afraid of.

I glanced into the snow behind him. "Was it only one? Or the brothers, too?"

"Just one."

"Do you think the others are waiting? That they'll rush us when I lift the gate?"

"If they do, I'll block the entrance again."

With ice. Nodding, I pushed up the lever. Erik came through, stripping off his bloodied shirt and wadding the shredded remains in his big hands. *God.* I knew he was big, tall. He'd held me against his broad chest and I'd seen the steely strength in his arms more than once before. But the whole package was completely unreal, heavy muscle sculpting a torso that I longed to touch. To taste. To wrap my arms around and hold on, feeling each muscle tighten and release as he moved deep inside me.

Heat surged beneath my skin. I averted my gaze, watching the gate as it lowered, but it was as if his image had been burned behind my eyes. I couldn't see anything else.

But I was aware of how he paused beside me. My breath was unsteady, and every nerve like a live wire. I didn't know what Erik saw when he looked at me. Hopefully not the need.

"You're shaking." His voice was bleak. "I'll go back out."

So trying to conceal my arousal only made me appear afraid of him. Great. "No. I just…" *What?* "I just keep expecting the others to come. The brothers."

At least it wasn't a lie.

Erik glanced out into the snow before shaking his head. "They can look like wolves, but it's not in a Hound's nature to fight in a pack. They probably all agreed to wait until the day after the solstice, just like they told us. But they won't."

"You'll think they'll attempt it individually, like this one did?"

"They'll want to one-up each other. To trick each other, not just us. I've heard they don't like to share."

So they won't want to share a victory. "But that's good, right? It's easier to take them out one at a time."

He swung the door closed. "Good and bad. We won't know when they're coming—and I'd rather stop them all at once and get you out of here."

Of course. I couldn't let myself forget the

reason why. "What's in a frost giant's nature, Erik?"

"We're not all the same."

"Then yours?"

His body stiffened, eyes paling to diamond. "Savage. Pure instinct and need."

Because of the frost giant or the curse? "Then what are you now?"

"Controlling it." His gaze narrowed, and my breath stopped as he abruptly stepped forward and caught my jaw in the cradle of his big hands, his skin feverishly hot. "You didn't answer me before. Are you all right?"

I didn't know if I was. A man—mostly—had just been killed outside this house. The man touching me had done it, blood still streaking his skin. And we had to deal with this curse.

"I'm not hurt," I finally said.

"That's not what I asked."

No, it wasn't. But I could ask him the same. "Are *you* all right? You just killed someone."

Even knowing it was necessary to defend himself after the Hound had shape-shifted and gone after him, that couldn't be easy.

Erik didn't answer for a long second. His gaze searched my face, his thumbs brushing over my cheekbones, and all at once he seemed almost tired, his expression weighed by worry.

"I'm not hurt," he said.

My smile probably looked as bleak and as weary as his. He watched me for a moment longer, then with a heavy breath released me. The heat of his touch gone, I immediately felt colder, shivering and wrapping my arms around myself.

I glanced at the door. "After you change clothes, do you think you can show me through the house, tell me if there are any bolt holes or fortified rooms?" In a fortress built for defense, there likely were a few. "Because they'll probably keep trying to attack you through me, and if I'm going to be waiting here by myself, I want to know where to hide if the Hounds find a way to get to me."

Erik's gaze snapped to mine, eyes burning. No longer tired, but tense and dangerous. "They won't get to you."

In this fortress? Probably not. But it was best to be prepared.

And his reaction gave me another reason. Suggesting the Hounds might attack me had transformed his bleak exhaustion into burning resolve. He stalked closer again, no longer visibly burdened by worry but determined to guard me with his body and life.

So maybe that was what we both needed: not to focus on what we couldn't change, but what we could. I wasn't above giving him another little push if I saw his worry return.

I wasn't above giving him another push now—but not too hard. Just a playful one. "Maybe the Hounds will come down the chimney," I said. "We should check it."

His eyes narrowed. "The chimney," he echoed.

"Yeah."

"Like Santa?"

"I was actually thinking of the Three Little Pigs. You know how the wolf says, 'Little pig, let me in' and the pigs say 'Not by the hair of my chinny-chin-chin'? And when the wolf can't blow down the brick house, he comes down the chimney." I pushed my fingers into my pockets, my heart leaping when Erik suddenly grinned. "I don't want to be the pig."

"You should," he said. "The pig won."

Oh, right. "In that case—Oink, oink."

"And in *that* case, I'd better take you into the kitchen and feed you."

That took a second to sink in, because he was closer now, just a few feet away, with amusement in his eyes, purpose in his every step, and so much bare skin on display. Absolutely gorgeous. Just watching him made my brain stumble a little, like an engine hiccuping before it turned over.

Then I realized what he'd said and gasped in mock outrage. But I really wanted to laugh, then cry, because that statement reminded me so much of the Erik who'd made my instincts jump up and shout "He's going to be The One!" like demented cheerleaders. It reminded me how easily he'd made me smile, and how much I'd liked him before he'd called our kiss a mistake and began looking at me with ice in his eyes.

But even though it reminded me of that Erik, there was a difference now, too—a warmth that hadn't been there a year and a half ago. Before, he'd made me laugh, but this was more personal. As if he knew my sense of humor well enough now that he felt comfortable teasing *me*—not just making some general, funny remark as he had before. As if he'd learned that much about me in the past eighteen months, even though we hadn't talked about anything except different construction projects. Maybe Erik hadn't been able to stop himself from paying attention to me any more than I'd been able to stop noticing him.

Hearing him tease me now made me wonder what might have been, if the curse hadn't screwed everything up. If he hadn't tried to protect me by staying away.

Then again, maybe the curse was the only reason he'd paid attention in the first place.

Erik's smile faded. "What is it?"

Nothing. Just a burning ache in my throat and a hollow pain in my chest. "I hate this curse," I said.

Darkness moved across his expression. "Not as much as I do."

Maybe not. It had to be close, though.

But I only nodded, because there was little else to do. And this conversation was veering toward 'dwelling on things we couldn't change.'

"Why don't you take me to the kitchen, then?" I picked up my bag from the sofa. "And show me where you keep the knives, just in case I need to stab the Hounds."

His eyes paled. "You won't need to. I'll never let them get to you."

God. Every time I suggested that the Hounds might, it was like watching some deadly, powerful warrior come to life within him—one who was determined to protect me. That wasn't the curse at all, I realized. That was Erik. He'd been trying to protect me for more than a year, beginning the night he'd kissed me. But now his control was thin and I was seeing what he usually hid.

If Erik's nature was to protect me and the Iron-wood witch's curse forced him to hurt me, then that only made the curse so much worse—forcing him to fight against himself instead of focusing on the Hound. It probably hadn't been so awful for his ancestors. What would they have cared if they fucked some random woman? A thousand years ago, many men believed that was all women were good for, anyway. Some still did. But not Erik. That was one of the things I'd liked about him from the very start. He hadn't dismissed me just because I was female.

But his need to protect me from himself and the need to protect me from the Hounds couldn't co-exist. Not as he'd decided they would.

"How are you going to stop them if I've shot you?"

Erik stilled, staring down at me. A battle seemed to wage through him, his jaw flexing as if he kept preventing himself from saying what he wanted to. I could almost feel his need to reassure me again, to declare that the Hounds would never touch me...but he couldn't promise that, because he wanted *me* to promise to kill him if we couldn't get out of here.

"The house will stop them," he finally said and took my hand, leading me toward a short hallway. His fingers burned against mine. I barely had a moment to savor the touch before he pulled his hand away and shoved his fists into his pockets. "But if it doesn't, you only need your gun. Shoot them as you would me."

I wasn't going to shoot Erik. But I might shoot the Hounds. "Why didn't you ask for my gun and shoot them all when we first saw them?"

"Because it wouldn't have done anything. It's always the same. A Hound can only tear out my throat and rip off my head. I can only kill one with a spear and by ripping his jaws open."

Sickness roiled in my gut. *Ripping his jaws open.* Erik had done that only a few minutes ago.

I tried not to imagine it—and was suddenly glad that the sheet of ice and the blizzard had saved me from seeing it. "But *I* can shoot a Hound in the head? Just like your uncle?"

"Yes."

"Then why didn't you ask *me* to shoot them?"

Erik stopped suddenly. A frown darkened his face. "I don't know. I never even considered it."

That wasn't like him. Coming up with solutions to problems was part of what Erik *did*—and he was usually very good at it. This would have all been over now if he had asked me to shoot the Hounds. I could have taken his truck and ran. Yet he hadn't even thought of that?

"You're not slow, Erik."

"No. But I could only think of getting you into the house. Of protecting you." His voice roughened. "Of how you'll taste."

My breath stopped.

Erik's eyes closed as if in dismay. "Jesus. I didn't intend to say—" His jaw clenched. "Forgive me, Olivia."

So telling me he wanted to taste me had just slipped out. That wasn't like him, either. Apparently it wasn't just his body that he had trouble controlling, but his thoughts, too.

Erik must hate that. But the Hounds must love it. "That's how the curse works, isn't it?" He wasn't really weakened. Just distracted. So focused on me that the Hounds could come up behind him.

"Yes."

"Well, when you get to the point where your brain is stuck between you legs, let me do the thinking."

A short laugh broke from him. "We might have a better shot of getting through this if you do."

"We *will* get through this. And it makes sense that you didn't have me shoot him," I said. "You went into default mode. You're the guy who is supposed to battle the Hounds, and the men in your family have for a thousand years, so it never occurred to you to ask me for any help. The house is here, it was built to protect anyone threatened by the Hounds, so it was the first and only route of action you considered. Your family planned for this, so you automatically followed that plan."

With his mouth flattened into a tight line, Erik nodded.

Pissed off at himself, not at me.

"Don't beat yourself up too much," I told him. "Even if you had asked me when we first saw them, I don't know if I would have shot one. And definitely not in the head. I'd have gone for a leg—or a body hit, if that didn't stop them."

But it wouldn't have.

"Don't beat myself up. Right." Erik suddenly stopped, looking down at me. His voice was rough. "I always dreaded meeting the woman who would trigger the curse. I couldn't imagine anything worse. For both of us."

So I was the worst thing to ever happen to him. But Erik wasn't the worst that ever happened to me.

Killing him would be.

I couldn't answer, though. His words had reached in and ripped apart something in my chest, and I couldn't breathe.

"But I still wondered what sort of woman she'd be." He spoke more softly now. "And you are incredible, Olivia. Searching for a fix. Trying so hard. And so brave in the face of all this. If I have to die, I'm glad it's for you."

The breath that had been locked in my chest shuddered free. "You're not going to die."

"I'll fight the curse, Olivia, but even if we manage to get you out of here, you have to be prepared—"

"*Don't* say it." I couldn't bear to hear again that I would have to shoot him.

His eyes closed. Jaw tight, he stood motionless for a long minute. Regaining control or fighting something else within him, I didn't know.

Finally he looked at me again, his eyes like hot ice. "I'm going upstairs to change. Then I'll feed you. Just wait for me in the kitchen. I'll show you the house afterward."

Silently, I nodded. My gaze followed his powerful stride as he turned toward the stairs and took three at a time. *Wait for him.*

No problem. I'd wait for him a lot longer than he probably realized.

CHAPTER SIX

SO I WAS FINALLY GETTING MY DINNER WITH ERIK. When I'd called him up eight months ago and asked him out, this wasn't really how I'd pictured it going. It was after midnight, and in the past twelve hours I'd only had half a protein bar; my hunger had returned with a growling vengeance, but anxiety held my throat so tight that I didn't know how I'd choke down a single bite. All the while, the curse would be hanging over our heads, a dead Hound lay outside somewhere, and two more were waiting to kill us.

And Erik and I would be…what? Trying to chat while we ate? I couldn't imagine how that would go, either.

But this wasn't a date. I couldn't let myself think of it like that. We were essentially in the middle of a siege. So we were just fueling up, preparing for battle. Literally, in Erik's case.

Unfortunately, pizza delivery wasn't an option this time. I didn't intend to make Erik cook for me, though—especially while laboring under a curse. I could at least get started while he changed clothes.

He was quicker than I anticipated. I'd only gotten as far as hanging my vest over the back of a barstool when he returned wearing a clean black t-shirt and jeans, his hair wet from the shower. He must not have spent much time drying off. Damp, the shirt clung to him as tightly as I wanted to.

But this *wasn't* a date. I pushed up my sleeves. "What do you want me to do?"

"Nothing. You'll sit. I'll feed you."

"I can help—"

His pale gaze caught mine. "Olivia." My name emerged on a growl, his voice tense and raw. "Let me take care of you."

God, the way he looked at me. His eyes burned with intensity, as if his need to feed me was as urgent as his need to protect me. As urgent as his need to fuck me.

Heart pounding, I nodded.

Erik turned away without a word, his shoulders rigid. Regaining his control again.

When some of the blue faded from his skin, I eased onto the stool. The knife I'd dropped earlier lay in front of me. Erik's blood stained the serrated edge.

I slid it across the countertop toward him. "You're going to use a different knife to chop stuff, right?"

A smile softened the hard lines of his mouth. "Right."

With a flick of his wrist, Erik tossed the knife into the sink and crossed to the built-in refrigerator—and suddenly, I didn't mind being relegated to the barstool. Not just because he was gorgeous, though that didn't hurt. I didn't even pretend to avert my gaze when he bent to slide open the freezer drawer and rummage around inside. Every single fantasy I had for the rest of my life would probably begin with Erik pulling steaks out of the fridge in his bare feet, a tight black t-shirt, and jeans that rode low on his hips.

I'd never gotten a chance to simply watch him; I'd always been working or trying *not* to look. And I'd never seen him at his own house. Maybe it shouldn't have surprised me that he seemed exactly the same here as in the office and on the job, where he always put every project in order before allowing anyone to dig a single shovelful of dirt. He approached cooking the same way. Every item he needed came out of the refrigerator and cupboards and was lined up on the counter, ready for use—a baguette, olive oil, smoked salmon, the steaks, and vegetables that I assumed would be tossed into a salad. Everything lay in order before he picked up a knife.

But I didn't just enjoy watching Erik because of the way he prepared for work. It was *him*, and how he filled the space he worked in, along with his easy way of moving that said he knew exactly what he was doing. On the job, that trait made people automatically look to him for answers and leadership; it was one of the first things that had attracted me to him. Now that same casual confidence was on display again. Of course he was at home here—but his familiarity with the kitchen told me that it wasn't just a space in his house. He knew exactly how to put it to use. And it would be so easy to sit like this for hours, watching him do exactly that.

It would be so easy to sit like this for a lifetime.

My chest tightened. I shouldn't start thinking of lifetimes and forever. Not with Erik. We'd both make it through the next few nights. We had to. But after the solstice, everything between us might go back to the way it had been before: with Erik glacial, and with me trying to forget him. He hadn't given me any reason to believe that it wouldn't.

Except...we *couldn't* return to how we'd been before. Because he'd left the firm. I wasn't going back to work, either. Not after John Gulbrandr sent me here to be raped. It didn't matter that I wanted Erik, and that if it came down to a choice between shooting him or having sex, I'd welcome a frost giant into my bed. His father couldn't have known that.

So after tonight, we'd have no connection at all. Not the firm, not a project. Only the curse. One night of fucking, once a year.

But I knew Erik would sever that connection, as well. Or at least try to control it and prevent himself from coming after me. He'd figure out a way to do it, too—no matter what it took. He wouldn't let something like this happen again.

I just hoped to God that this time next year I wouldn't be sitting around like a lovesick idiot, waiting for a frost giant to knock down my front door.

Jesus. Forget next year. I was sitting around

like a lovesick idiot *now*. He stood at the stovetop grill toasting thin slices of baguette, and instead of trying to find out more about the curse, I was admiring the impressive breadth of his shoulders.

I needed to get my head on straight. "You said your dad wasn't affected by the curse. Did he have to fight a Hound, too?"

Erik glanced at me, then his attention returned to the grill and he flicked the little pieces of toast onto a plate. "He defeated one about thirty years ago."

When Erik had been five years old. "Did you see it happen?"

"Yes." His voice flattened. "He came during the summer. We were outside. It was quick."

And bloody, I imagined. But Erik didn't describe it and I wasn't going to ask. Instead I thought over the timeline while he worked at the other counter. "Is it a generational thing? Son versus son?"

"Technically. But some of my ancestors have faced two or three in their lifetimes."

"For the same reason that you are—because the others come to avenge their fathers or brothers?" I asked, and Erik nodded. "Does the eldest-son bit apply to your family, too? If you had a younger brother, would he have to worry about the curse?"

"He would if I died before fathering a son. Then my brother would be the eldest."

Just the suggestion made my chest ache. But Erik *wasn't* going to die. This was all just hypothetical. "But you don't have a brother or son."

"No. So if I die, the curse jumps to a cousin's line. It's happened before. The Gulbrandrs are sons of Odin's sons, but not everyone has been the son of an eldest son. That uncle who was shot in the head—he was an eldest. Then the curse jumped to my line."

"So there really is no end to the feud. It just leaps to another branch on the family tree."

"Until Ragnarök."

Hopefully that wouldn't be happening anytime soon. "So your sons will have to fight a Hound, too. At least the oldest one will."

"Yes. And I'll train them as my father did me— to protect them as best I can." His shoulders stiffened. "But I sure as hell wouldn't do everything the same way."

"Like sending me here?" And refusing to shatter his bones again.

"Yes. And if my son begged me to help protect a woman that he—" Abruptly, Erik shook his head, cutting himself off. Body rigid, he stood utterly still, and his deep, ragged inhalations filled the tense silence. When he spoke again, the bleak pain in his voice twisted my heart into a knot. "I'd do it for him. But it doesn't matter. I won't be having a son. When I come after you, you'll have to stop me, and my line will end."

No, it wouldn't. But I couldn't get a word past the lump in my throat, and I was suddenly glad Erik faced the other way. This was all hypothetical. I shouldn't have been fighting tears. Thankfully, he didn't seem in a hurry to turn around, and after a few seconds I managed to gather myself together again.

But no more hypotheticals. At least none that included any scenario in which Erik died. "You said your family usually wins. So why aren't the Hounds wiped out by now? At some point, there just aren't any more branches in the tree."

"You'd think so." Erik glanced back, his pale eyes unreadable. "But the Moon Hound's sons generate a lot of twigs. They're born in litters of ten."

I sputtered. Litters? God. So awful, yet so funny to imagine. "Are you serious?"

"No. I needed to see you laugh." He slid a plate in front of me. "This should hold you until the rest is ready."

I glanced down. Five crostini formed a flower on the plate, each petal topped by a near-translucent slice of smoked salmon. Disbelief parted my lips. "You just made this?"

But I knew he had. I'd ogled his perfect ass while he'd done it.

"I did," he confirmed. "I put it together, anyway. I had most of it ready."

"It's so pretty." A dollop of thick, herbed yogurt lay beneath the salmon. I spied the container on the counter—not store-bought, but something he'd mixed up. I touched my fingertip to it and tasted. Lemon and dill. Absolutely delicious. I hesitated before pulling the plate closer and digging in. "Are we sharing?"

He shook his head. "I had a man-sized version for lunch."

Man-sized? I questioned that with a lift of my brows, because my mouth was already full and my taste buds were dying a happy little death.

"A hunk of bread, a chunk of salmon. Nothing so dainty." His diamond gaze settled on my lips. "All right?"

I nodded—but the truth was, I didn't know. When he looked at me like that, I didn't taste anything at all. I could only see his wide, firm lips.

I could only remember the slick heat of our kiss. God, I wanted him. I wanted him to come across the counter and fill me up, to ease the desperate hunger that would never be satisfied by food.

Only by Erik.

My voice was husky when I finally swallowed. "These will definitely keep me until dinner. And I suppose that will take a while."

"About twenty minutes," he said. "Longer if you want yours well-done."

"Medium rare." But even that would take longer than twenty minutes. "You're not going to throw them on the grill while they're frozen, are you?"

"They're not frozen."

"You just took them out—"

I broke off when he unwrapped the butcher paper and revealed two thawed filets. But how...?

Oh. Frost giant.

"Show off," I said.

His grin made my heart skip. "A little."

"I imagine you don't get many chances to." I licked a bit of yogurt from my thumb and reached for another crostini. Meat sizzled when he laid it on the grill, and the mouth-watering scent was already filling the kitchen when he returned to the island. "So there are some positives to the frost giant thing?"

Smile vanishing, he shook his head. "Not any that are worth the negative."

The curse. "But if the curse hadn't jumped to your line?"

"There'd be more positives." His steady gaze met mine. "But the curse *did* jump. I can't escape that."

No one could escape something like that when it came for them. "I used to be envious of my mom—I used to wish that I hadn't been in the skipped generation. I still am a little envious. But at the same time, I'm glad I don't have to make the decisions that she does. How to use her ability…and how *not* to use it. I guess magic is always double-edged."

"Yes," he agreed softly.

And the only thing to do was try to blunt those edges and protect the people around them. As my mother did. As Erik tried to protect me. As his grandfather had tried to protect his wife by building this fortress.

But not just a wife. His *family*. And someone else must have taken that one step further, because I was pretty sure the layout of the kitchen, family seating area, and dining room hadn't always been so open. Someone had knocked down walls, so whoever worked in the kitchen wouldn't be separated from the activity at the heart of the house. Not just protecting the family, but bringing them together.

They'd done it seamlessly, too. The construction was flawless. I couldn't be certain that there *had* been a change in the original layout until I studied the kitchen again. Stainless steel. Sandstone brick. More river rock under the hood. Some old, but lots of new. "Your grandfather built this house. But this kitchen isn't from the fifties or sixties."

"No."

I eyed the built-in refrigerator, the gas range, and the double ovens. All top-of-the-line appliances that would probably still look modern three decades from now. "It was remodeled about ten years ago?"

"Yes." A lick of flame flared up as he turned over a steak. "When my grandfather died, I took over the house and redesigned this part of it."

"Your dad didn't? It's not a family home?"

"It is. But my father isn't affected by the curse."

And didn't need to rely on the house to protect him and Erik's mother during the solstice. "You weren't affected by it ten years ago."

"No. But the possibility was there." His jaw tightened, and he didn't need to say the rest: That possibility had been realized. "So the house is mine. I have a loft in Denver, but this is mine."

Not just owned, but *his*. "It fits you." Big, solid, and designed to protect. "Like this room. I can't tell you how many times I've built houses with a kitchen like this, just because the owners have the money, but half of them would never step foot into it. You know your way around one, though. It's not just for show."

I didn't think anything about this house—or Erik—was for show. There was too much strength and purpose in both.

"You can thank my mother." A faint smile touched his mouth as he set the steaks aside to rest. "She insisted I learn."

I picked up the last crostini. "So that you could take care of yourself?"

"So that I could give someone at least one reason to marry me."

The toast caught in my throat, choking me. *One* reason? I could see a million reasons why someone would want to.

Coughing, I tried to swallow. Erik shoved a glass of water into my hand and watched me sip, his diamond eyes glittering and his knuckles white.

"You're all right?" His voice sounded as rough

as my throat felt.

I nodded and managed to catch my breath. "I just laughed at the wrong time. Your mom really didn't think they'd have a reason?"

"Not the usual one."

What was the usual one? Love? Kids? Companionship? Sex?

But those wouldn't be Erik's primary concern, I realized. The worst thing he'd imagined was meeting the woman who triggered the curse. So he would put finding someone who didn't trigger it before all of the usual reasons.

That completely ruled me out. No wonder he'd filed me away as a mistake and turned me down for dinner. Not just to protect me. I was the opposite of what he'd been looking for.

My gaze fell to my empty plate. I wasn't choking anymore, but the ache in my throat wouldn't go away. "So she wanted you to find some nice girl and convince her that you'd at least be useful in the kitchen?"

"Yes."

I would have taken him for that reason. And so many others. So why *wasn't* he taken? "Is the frost giant thing a hard sell?"

"I don't know. I've never tried to sell it."

"But you would tell her, right? Did your mom know before she married your dad?"

"Yes. To both." Porcelain scraped over the counter as he abruptly cleared away my plate and crossed to the sink. "He told her exactly why he was marrying her."

"I guess that wasn't for the usual reason, either?"

"No. With her, he didn't risk the curse. He liked and respected her. And she could give him children."

"That's pretty cold." And I'd been right about the priorities. All the usual reasons were there—kids, companionship—but love was glaringly missing. So was sex, but considering that they'd made one child, it must have been included.

"It was practical. It was what my mother wanted, too. She had a bad first marriage. She was just looking for stability and friendship, not romance."

"That makes sense, I guess." It wasn't what I wanted. But I understood it. And I supposed it was better than lying to a woman and letting her believe he was marrying for love. "So they're not in love with each other. They're just…partners."

"Yes." He bit off the word as if it tasted bad.

Suddenly uncertain, I studied him. He stood at the sink and I couldn't see his expression, but his body had tensed—his spine rigid and the muscles in his arms sharply defined. When he rinsed my plate beneath the faucet, icy claws tipped his long fingers.

"Erik," I said softly. "Are you losing control, or are you pissed off?"

Eyes burning with blue flame, he shot me a look over his shoulder. "I'm in control."

So he was angry. "Is it because I'm asking all of this personal stuff?"

"No. I think he's a goddamn fool."

"Your dad?"

"Yes." He twisted the water off. "It's not something a man can control. He can try. *I* tried. But it still happened. It could for him, too. Then he'll just end up hurting her."

Hurt Erik's mom, I realized. No wonder he was pissed if he was thinking about that. "You mean, if your dad met someone and the curse caught up to him?"

"Not someone else. It could be her. He can't know."

"She has witch's blood, too?"

"No."

"But…" Completely confused, I shook my head. Somehow I'd gotten all mixed up. First I'd believed the kiss had triggered the curse, then I'd been under the impression that having witch blood in me was the reason. But it *had* to be more complicated, I realized—because John Gulbrandr had met me and he wasn't compelled to fuck me.

Thank God for that.

So what had triggered it? *None* of this seemed to make sense. John Gulbrandr had married Erik's mother because she hadn't triggered the curse, yet she still could in the future?

And given everything else Erik had told me, his anger didn't make sense, either. "You said you were going to do the same thing: find a nice girl, woo her with food, then marry her for practical reasons."

"I'm a fucking idiot, too." He regarded me with a pale, brooding gaze. "What if I had? Then I meet you. And this still happens."

Making a horrible situation even worse. Thanks to the curse, the men in his family had a few shitty choices and fewer good ones. I could be angry with John Gulbrandr for a lot of reasons, and I thought the way he'd chosen to marry was as cold as hell… but the alternative was never having a family or a son. I couldn't blame him for wanting both.

I wouldn't have blamed Erik, either. But he must not have been in a rush to marry, because he could have a long time ago. Yet he hadn't.

Thank God for that, too.

"It would've been pretty terrible all around if you had a wife," I agreed. "On the bright side, though—if the curse forced you to cheat on her, you wouldn't have so much trouble finding someone to shoot you."

Erik stared at me for a long second. He didn't reply, but by the slow smile widening his mouth, I guessed that my response had broken through his anger. He gathered our plates from beside the grill.

"Do you mind eating here or do you prefer the dining table?"

"I'm comfortable here." And not in a hurry to move.

He didn't seem in a hurry to sit. After setting my steak in front of me, he placed his plate at the end of the island. Not pulling up his own barstool, but standing at the corner of the cabinet—facing me from about two feet away, with his fists shoved into his pockets.

"I don't think it's a good idea for me to get too comfortable," he said softly. "Or too close."

"So that when the Hound breaks in, you can save me?"

"Right," he said—and, God, his grin just made me want to lick him all over. "You worked out a fix, didn't you?"

"What?"

"You mention the Hound and I regain a little control. Just like saying a magic word."

I hadn't realized it affected his control; I'd only noticed that it redirected his focus away from fucking me and toward defending me.

But maybe that was essentially the same thing. "Will it help us through the solstice?"

"I don't know. But it helps for now."

So if he began to slip again, I had to tell him that the Hound was out there, hoping to get in and tear me apart. Until telling him didn't work anymore.

I took a sip of water and his pale gaze fell to my glass. "Do you prefer wine?" he asked. "I have some red."

"No. It might ruin my aim when the Hound comes for me." When he laughed and his tension seemed to ease a little more, I said, "So after two more nights, this will all be over. Since you're not at the firm anymore, what do you intend to do?"

His smile disappeared. "God, Olivia. You're so damned—"

"Optimistic? Foolish? Pigheaded?"

He sighed and shook his head. "Incredible."

I liked it when he gave in to the inevitable. We

would get through this. I picked up my steak knife. "So what will you do?"

"Find work out of the country. Europe. Australia. I don't know."

My chest suddenly felt heavy, as if my lungs were lined with lead. *Everything* felt heavy and oddly detached. I watched my blade slice through the steak, but I wasn't hungry anymore and I couldn't make myself look up at him. "So far away?"

"It has to be far enough that I can't get to you. I should have done it this year. Booked a flight and left, instead of thinking that not knowing where you were would be good enough."

"You can't fly out next year? A lot of people leave over the holidays."

"I don't want to take that risk. There are too many things that could go wrong. Weather. Some mechanical problem. If another Hound shows up and stops me from leaving."

"Then give yourself more room for error. Or go back and forth over the equator every six months. Avoid the winter solstice entirely."

"Others have tried that. But it hits them during the northern solstice even if it's summer in the south. So it's better just to go as far as I can and stay there."

Or you could just stay here. But that wasn't the choice he'd made. So I didn't let myself say it and forced my way through chewing and swallowing. "And if the curse wasn't a factor? What would you do?"

Erik didn't immediately respond. The silence drew out, and I realized that he wasn't pausing to finish a bite before speaking, as I'd assumed. Glancing up, I saw that he hadn't even touched his plate. His fists were still balled in his pockets.

My gaze rose to his face. He was watching me, and the anguished longing in his gaze seemed to punch me in the throat.

"Erik?" I whispered.

As if the sound of my voice hurt him, he closed his eyes. His jaw clenched. Another long second passed before he said, "I'd start my own firm."

He was answering my question, I realized. I'd almost forgotten that I'd asked him what he would do if the curse hadn't erased so many of his choices.

"Your *own* firm? Not partnering with your dad again?"

"No. Maybe with…someone else."

"Someone who isn't such an asshole?" I asked, and he nodded, amusement briefly lightening his expression. "What else would you do?"

The bleakness returned. "The usual."

The usual. Love. Kids and companionship.

My stomach tightened into a sick knot and I had to glance away from him. Suddenly, I understood what had put that anguished look on his face, and why he hadn't been in a rush to marry. Erik might have told himself that he would find a wife for practical reasons...but that wasn't what he'd *wanted.*

I don't know why I hadn't seen it before. But it was right here, all around me, staring me in the face. Ten years ago, he'd remade these rooms for a family. Why bother, unless some part of him had wanted the usual? That would have started with love. But with the threat of the curse hanging over him, he probably wouldn't have risked falling in love, only to see it destroyed when he was forced to fuck another woman. And he wouldn't make the same decisions that his father had. So he'd been left with a life that might have at least been satisfying, if not everything he'd dreamed. He could have built his own firm, had friends and success. But now the curse threatened to take the rest, too.

No life, no future.

Because he'd met me.

It wasn't my fault. I knew it wasn't. But knowing

I'd been the catalyst tore me up. And while he watched his life fall apart, I'd been stuffing my face and staring at his ass.

I set my knife down. I couldn't eat another bite—but Erik wasn't eating, either.

I glanced at his plate, still untouched, then up to his face. My breath locked in my throat.

No more anguish. Just blazing need, with his pale blue gaze fixed on my lips.

Oh, God. I had to mention the Hound and help him regain control. But I didn't want to. Instead I wanted Erik's hands on my skin, his mouth on mine, and his cock deep inside me. I wanted him to fulfill the burning promise in his eyes.

I would just have to touch him. I'd just have to move closer, and the tenuous hold he had on himself would break, and I would know.

And I hated myself for even thinking it. If we were down to no other choice—sex or shooting him—that would have been different. But I *did* have a choice now, and taking advantage of the curse to get what I wanted would be unforgivable.

So I said the magic word. "Has your family ever tried to negotiate with the Hounds, to find a solution that stops people from dying on both sides?"

"A few times." His focus didn't shift away from

my mouth. "My great-grandfather was friends with one—until that Hound was compelled to attack him."

"Did your great-grandfather win?"

"Yes."

"That must have been difficult, killing a friend." Difficult killing anyone, even if they'd attacked first. "I don't think the brothers are interested in a truce. That was pretty obvious from the second they destroyed my Jeep, then taunted us with my under-wear."

Now that one of the brothers was dead, I suspected there was no hope at all that this could be resolved—except with more death.

His gaze finally snapped up to meet mine. "We're not sorry to destroy some of them." It was a low growl. "I'll get your panties back for you and rip off the Hound's arms for touching them."

"That's okay." I didn't want them back. And I might have laughed, because it was absurd—going out to fight the Hounds for underwear—but tension wormed its way down the back of my neck and my heart began to pound.

Instincts? Or because his words reminded me of how violent and bloody his confrontation with the Hounds would be? Had *already* been. I wasn't sure. But I couldn't catch my breath. The t-shirt stretched across Erik's broad chest seemed to be tighter now and the fists balled in his pockets didn't conceal the thick ridge behind his zipper.

I'd said the magic words, I'd reminded him that the Hound was waiting out there, yet Erik wasn't regaining control.

Like pale blue flames, his gaze returned to my mouth again. I couldn't stop the response of my body to that look, the clenching need, the shiver over my skin that left my nipples tight and aching. Would it be now? Losing control, coming closer— taking me right here.

Oh, my God. How could this arouse me? Yet I could feel my flesh readying for him, the sudden ache and wet.

Maybe that was the witch's blood, too. But maybe magic wasn't the reason at all. Maybe it was just Erik—and me, because I'd wanted him for so long.

But right now, it was wrong. Not my response. Just the part of me that considered letting this go further when he had so little choice in the matter.

"Erik."

Only a single strained whisper, but it got through to him. His eyes closed and although he didn't move, I felt his withdrawal in the new tension that claimed his form.

He didn't look at me as he said, "I need to track down another Hound."

Because as soon as he did, we could risk leaving in his truck.

Except that we couldn't. Not with the blizzard raging. Erik might be able to clear the roads but the whole point of that escape was to draw out the final Hound so that I could drive on alone. Driving through this storm might be more dangerous than staying.

But I wouldn't raise any doubts about that plan now. It was the only one we had—and by the time the second Hound was dead, the storm might have blown over.

Hoarsely he continued, "I won't come back in until either the second Hound is dead or my control is slipping, because I can't risk coming through the walls and giving them a way in."

Then he believed I might shoot him. My throat an aching knot, I only nodded.

So this was it. The next time I saw him, we'd either be risking an escape from here and I'd be running as far away as I could, or we'd be forced to make a terrible decision—to shoot him or to risk taking a frost giant to my bed.

And if it came to that, I didn't think we'd make the same choice.

Chapter Seven

Erik should have fixed the insulation in his roof when he'd remodeled. Outside the south tower room window, enormous icicles hung from the eaves. Each one was six to seven feet long, several inches thick at the top and tapering to a dangerous point. I usually only saw these kind of icicles on cheaply-built houses and apartment buildings; I'd never have expected them in one of the Gulbrandrs' homes. They were an indication that too much heat escaped the house through the roof, melting the snow piled on top. Now the hanging ice gave the impression of a cage bars. Not keeping me in. Keeping danger out.

Somehow the icicles had survived the blasting

wind...so far. The storm had continued through the night, whistling past the windows of the north tower room. I'd tossed uneasily in bed until the early hours, when exhaustion had finally knocked me out. It was almost noon when I'd woken.

Outside, there was nothing but white. Although the blizzard didn't seem as fierce now, the driving snow reduced visibility to about ten yards beyond the window. Every once in a while the wind subsided briefly and I caught a glimpse of the trees at the edge of the clearing.

I didn't catch any glimpses of Erik, though I'd spent most of my time at the windows searching for him, with worry a constant weight in my chest.

We hadn't lowered the portcullis this time. Instead Erik had filled the gatehouse with a huge block of ice that he could easily pass through, but the Hounds couldn't. Erik hadn't needed to explain why. If he lost control out there, he'd come through the ice instead of destroying the gate. He wanted to be certain that I could still keep the Hounds out after I'd shot him.

I didn't plan to. I'd rather shoot the Hounds if they came in after him. Of course, I didn't know how I'd manage firing a gun if Erik was screwing me. Being banged by a frost giant could probably fuck up anyone's aim.

God, this was *all* so fucked up.

I pressed my forehead against the freezing pane. My breath fogged the glass. Still no sign of Erik.

Was he all right out there? Obviously he didn't think the cold would hurt him—and neither would losing sleep and going without something to eat. But two Hounds who wanted to kill him were waiting out there somewhere, too.

Why hadn't we thought to establish a signal of some sort, just to verify that he was okay? Stupid. Then again, if the Hounds caught on to the signal, they might use it against us. Try to trick us again.

I just had to be patient and calm. Easier said than done, and the solstice was still more than a full day away. This uncertainty was already driving me crazy, and I felt absolutely useless in here.

So I needed to make myself useful. Only one way to do that—by combating uncertainty with knowledge.

Shivering, I forced myself away from the window. Each tower room had its own fireplace— not as grand as the fireplace downstairs, but one that did the job just as well. I'd lit the fire in the north tower room before I'd fallen asleep last night, but the south tower room was still chilly. Erik's room.

My gaze shot to the oversized bed dominating the chamber. Bigger than king-sized, the mattress was huge. Made for a giant. The black walnut posts at each corner appeared hand carved. Not by Erik—the bed was too old—but maybe his grandfather. The old framed photograph propped on the nightstand was probably of him. Captured in fading color, a big, smiling man stood with his arm circling the waist of a dark-haired woman in a sundress, who held a toddler on her hip. The fortress sprawled behind them; this tower was visible in the upper corner.

I studied the woman for a long moment. His grandfather had built this house for her, Erik had said, and his grandfather had also suffered from the curse. For at least a moment, however, neither appeared to be suffering. The photo had caught them looking into each other's eyes instead of at the camera. A breeze had swept a curl across her forehead, and she seemed on the edge of a laugh, her expression bright and his adoring.

The toddler—most likely Erik's dad—was about eighteen months old. So she'd probably already been through at least a couple of solstices at that point. Maybe two or three, or even more. I didn't know how long they'd been married before John Gulbrandr had been born.

Despite everything Erik had told me about the curse, there was still too much that I didn't know. And something else was nagging at me, too—and had been since my conversation with Erik over dinner. There'd been something, *something* that hadn't made sense, and I'd meant to ask him about it...but then I'd been distracted and it had slipped away. I could remember needing to ask but couldn't remember what the question was.

But it was nagging at me again now, as if this picture of his grandparents had brought my mind back around to that question. I just couldn't nail down what it had been.

The books might help. I replaced the photo and began examining the titles. There were a lot of them. Floor-to-ceiling shelves filled two walls of Erik's room. I didn't know if his house in the city was the same, but it was easy to imagine him sitting up in bed at night with a book in his hand. Smart men didn't get that way in a vacuum. I skimmed over biographies, histories—many of them related to our field—and a few paperback mysteries and thrillers that I'd read. His personal library looked a lot like mine, except more substantial.

A section on Norse mythology took up four shelves. I didn't know where to start. But I had nothing except time.

I grabbed four books and headed back to the north tower room—the only heated chamber in the house. Shampoo in the connecting bathroom and a few items in the closet made me suspect that the room was usually his mother's when she visited. I might end up having to borrow some of her clothes before this was—

The woman who triggered the curse didn't have to have witch's blood.

That was it. That was what I'd forgotten to ask about. Because I'd thought that was what Erik had told me in the gatehouse—that a witch or her offspring triggered the curse. But Erik's mother wasn't one, and he'd said that she might trigger the curse in his dad, too. She just hadn't yet.

So what really caused it? Did they even know?

Rolling it around in my head, I settled into the loveseat facing the fire and piled the books onto the cushion beside me. I let them sit for a minute. The curse's starting point wasn't the only thing nagging at me.

The curse itself just didn't make *sense*.

Who was most hurt by it? The woman. Yet supposedly the witch of the Ironwood had cursed the *men* in Erik's family. So why weren't they the ones being raped or tortured or torn apart?

And it just wasn't practical. If the point was to give the Hounds a chance to win on the solstice, then why were some of the frost giants exempt? Why didn't the curse hit all of them? Yet it had never affected Erik's dad. So either the rules of the curse changed as the years passed, or the rule was something I just hadn't figured out yet.

Except that whatever the rule was, it was stupid. Erik could have easily freed himself from the curse just by killing me. Not that *he* would. But unless the Gulbrandrs and their ancestors were the most innately decent men who ever lived, no way could I believe that some wouldn't have taken the easy way out. When the Hounds showed up at their door, the frost giants would have ripped the woman's head off to save themselves.

Since Erik's dad sent me here to be raped, I suspected that I could cross out 'innately decent.'

But even if the Hounds weren't an issue, guilt and fear wouldn't always be, either. Erik was tortured by the thought of what he might do. Not everyone would be. Hell, some human men used a short skirt as an excuse to force themselves on women. How easy would it be to shift blame and guilt when *magic* forced them to rape someone?

So it all came back around to the same problem: the curse was far more likely to hurt the woman than any son of Odin's son.

Which meant that either I was still ignorant of some vital information regarding the curse, or the witch of the Ironwood was the most shortsighted and ineffectual witch ever. If I was ever going to curse someone, I'd make certain he couldn't escape the suffering. I'd go straight for his balls.

Or his heart.

Something stilled inside me. Blindly I stared into the fireplace, not seeing the flames but imagining exactly how I'd aim a curse at a man's heart. There were a few certain ways to do it—either hurt those he loved…or make *him* hurt those he loved.

That would be a really, really vicious curse.

God. I pushed my hands into my hair, pulling until my scalp hurt, trying to make my brain work harder. Was I really thinking this? But I couldn't stop remembering that photo of Erik's grandparents.

There'd been love there. It had practically beamed out of their faces. And Erik said his grandfather had been broken when she'd died. But his grandfather hadn't been the one to hurt her. She'd survived twenty solstices. Even though he'd been so big, and she'd been so small.

His father and mother weren't in love, though. And John Gulbrandr wasn't affected by the curse.

Erik was.

My chest felt tight; I could hardly breathe. There was only one direction that all of this was leading, and my instincts were screaming that I was on the right track, but I couldn't even bear to face the answer squarely. What if it was just hormones again—or wishful thinking? I'd been so wrong before.

My heart wouldn't survive being wrong again. Not about this.

So I had to put it aside. The reason Erik was cursed didn't matter. Not really. It didn't change the effect it was having on Erik now, or that the solstice would be upon us tomorrow night. Sitting here, obsessing over a question that I couldn't answer wouldn't solve any of our problems.

Maybe the books would.

* * *

WHAT LITTLE I DISCOVERED ABOUT the Ironwood witch didn't make her sound like a woman who'd create a weak or ineffectual curse. One book called her a giantess, another a troll. All of them mentioned her relationship with Loki, and that she'd borne a son, Fenrir the Wolf—the Hounds' ancestor—but a few also claimed that she was mother to two more of Loki's children: Hel, who ruled the hall of the dead, and Jörmungandr, an enormous serpent who surrounded the world in his coils and whose poison would kill Thor during Ragnarök. That was a witch with one hell of a legacy and bloodline.

Unfortunately, knowing that didn't help Erik and me now. Nor did anything else I found in the books. I kept my nose between the pages until dark, then heated up soup from the pantry and ate while reading more.

But by the time I prepared for bed, I wasn't even reading anymore. Instead I was just keeping my eyes busy, because otherwise I'd be standing at the window and staring out into the driving snow. Not a word from or a glimpse of Erik all day. I eventually fell into a fitful sleep and woke late the next morning.

The day of the solstice brought rabid anxiety that chewed holes in my gut. Lying in bed, I mechanically turned pages and scanned words and didn't have a clue what I read. I examined every woodcut and illustration as if the drawings might offer some magical hint of what was happening outside.

At noon, I made myself get up and shower. My underwear was still drying over the towel rack and I didn't want to put my jeans back on without them. None of the shirts in his mother's closet fit comfortably, so I stole a blue sweater from Erik's closet instead. On me, it was more like a sweater-dress. Wrapped in its warmth and wearing a thick pair of socks, I carried the books I'd read back to his room and began reshelving them. My gaze skimmed the remaining titles, but I didn't feel like taking another back to the north tower room.

There were no answers on these shelves. Nothing that could save us. If there had been, surely Erik would have already discovered it.

God, and where was he? Was he all right?

I moved to the window. Still snowing. The wind wasn't so constant and terrible now, but came in gusts that twisted the falling snowflakes into wild flurries. A few of the enormous icicles had snapped off. Most still remained, like heavy spears of ice dangling from the eaves.

Still no sign of him. No movement in the snow.

Fighting despair, I forced myself back to the shelves. It didn't matter if the books helped me understand the curse or frost giants. A distraction was the only way I'd get through the next hours. It was only afternoon and my stomach was already a sick, knotted ache.

I just needed to know if Erik was okay.

My eyes burned. Blindly I pulled a thick paperback novel from the nearest shelf. A thriller. Some killer was targeting women. Jesus, I didn't care. The mystery would be solved and there would be a happy ending for everyone except the dead women, and there was no way I could focus on this when Erik was out there. Maybe a movie or—

The hairs on the back of my neck prickled. Had I heard something from downstairs? I wasn't sure. Now there was only the gusting wind. Holding my breath, I listened.

Over the thundering of my heart came a faint rattle. The portcullis.

Sudden joy burst through the anxiety and I spun away from the shelves. That only meant one thing. Erik was back. Erik was—

Here. In the room.

Shock yanked me to a skidding halt. My socks slipped on the stone floor. He moved *so* fast, big hands catching me around the waist. Heat radiated off him. His t-shirt and jeans were soaked—not in blood this time, but melted snow. Pulse racing, I stared up into his face, trying to take everything in at once. Blue skin. The unmistakable ridge of his erection. The diamond glow in his intense, ravenous gaze.

Oh, my God. My body instantly responded to that look, as if the heat of his skin sank through mine, warming my flesh.

"Erik." I only managed a strained whisper. "Did you kill a Hound?"

The magic word. I was almost sorry for using it when he closed his eyes and let go of my waist—but he didn't go far. He gripped the shelves beside my shoulders. Still surrounding me.

Clutching the paperback to my chest, I didn't move. Didn't do anything that might be construed as running away.

No matter how much a part of me wanted to.

"I didn't find them." His voice was gravel and ice, his teeth sharp. "But I can't risk staying outside now."

Because his control was thin. Because he might come through the walls to get me.

My breath shuddering, I nodded. "You closed

the portcullis, right? So the Hounds can't get in?"

A low growl rumbled through his chest and emerged as a single word. "Yes."

"And this *is* you? Not the Hounds tricking me? How do I know?"

His gaze met mine again. Still diamond, still hot, but I must have been getting through to him. His need to protect me and to reassure me was battling with his need to have me—and for now, protection was winning out.

I didn't know how long it would.

"The Mueller Park project," he said roughly. "It's going to come in at almost twenty million over budget."

My relieved grin was ridiculously wide. "The taxpayers won't be happy."

"The governor's next opponent will."

I laughed, but it faded as his smile slowly tightened and new torment filled his eyes. Still battling himself. And judging by the thick spear of his cock behind denim, more than ready to fuck me.

I should have been afraid. I knew that. He'd begged me to put a bullet in his head to prevent him from hurting me...but I simply couldn't imagine that he would. I'd kicked him in the balls, and the worst he'd done was drop me. Even if he lost control now and screwed me against the bookshelf, I couldn't imagine it being painful—and all at once, I could easily imagine loving every hard surge of his body into mine.

Liquid warmth spread through me as I pictured it: my legs wrapped around his hips, his heavy muscles bunching under my fingers. Heat and ice.

I must be insane. My gaze lifted to his.

The skin across his cheekbones paled. White edged his lips. "Don't look at me like that," he said hoarsely.

I couldn't help it. "How should I look?"

"Terrified." His gaze dropped to my mouth. "Ready to run."

But I wasn't. "Why do you think you'll hurt me?"

"God, Olivia. If you could see what is in my head, you wouldn't have to ask that." On either side of me, his carved biceps flexed; I heard the ice surrounding his hands crack. White-hot, his diamond gaze seared mine. "If you could feel how I need to be inside you. If you knew how I'd tear apart mountains to come after you. How I'd destroy anyone that stood in my way. All just to have you. Nothing is safe from me—especially you, if you're under me. I won't have control."

No control. Knowing that didn't scare me as much as Erik probably imagined. His words made it impossible to think of anything *but* being under him, of losing control with him as he fucked me deep and hard. I forced myself to concentrate past the need pulsing through my body.

Holding his gaze, I took a deep breath. "I'm willing to take that risk."

"No." It was sharp, hoarse.

"I get it, Erik. You don't want to hurt me." My fingers tightened on the book clutched to my chest. "But I don't want to hurt you, either. So why is it better for me to shoot you?"

Another growl tore from him. "Because I'll be attacking you. You'll be defending yourself. It's not equal."

"It's equal if neither of us is hurt and we both make it through the solstice okay. Your grandmother was fine. What if it's not as bad as you think?"

"Not every woman that my ancestors have taken was fine. And you see me like *this*, Olivia. As a man. But I'll be different." Harsh desolation lined his face. "You haven't seen me…and what I can do."

Such as ripping a Hound apart. Maybe he was right. Maybe I was just fooling myself, believing that we'd be all right.

Throat thick, I nodded. My eyes burned as I turned to put the book away.

The ice around his arms shattered. All at once Erik dragged me back against his chest, his left forearm locked around my waist. The book tumbled from my fingers. Gasping, I struggled for balance, gripping the edge of a shelf for support, trying not to feel the hardness of his cock wedged against my ass.

"Erik?"

His body shuddered. He was fighting for control, I realized.

And losing.

His fevered skin burned the length of my bare thigh as his right hand slid beneath the hem of the sweater. My heart stopped. Frozen by shock and anticipation, I shook as his hand traveled higher, and suddenly there was nothing in the world but his touch, his palm curving around my hip, his fingers diving between my thighs, where my flesh was wet and swollen with need.

He abruptly stilled. I squeezed my eyes shut, my face heating. He couldn't possibly mistake my arousal.

His tortured groan broke the silence. "I did this to you?"

He'd always been able to do this to me. "Just ignore it," I said desperately. "And I will, too."

"Ignore it? You might as well ask me to move the moon. You're in need, Olivia." Gently, he slicked his fingers over my clitoris. My hips jerked involuntarily and I bent my head, clenching my teeth to stop my moan. "And I need to ease it for you."

Oh, God. I wanted him to. But his control was already slipping. "How, Erik? With a little rub and a tickle?" Each word was sharp. "Because it won't be enough for me. And you already said that fucking is off the table. Will it be enough for you? Enough for the curse?"

Erik stiffened behind me. A harsh, cold breath against my ear was his only response. Maybe he couldn't manage any more.

But his fingers were still rubbing, gliding over my clit before pushing deeper to tease at my entrance—then sliding back up to do it all over again.

Though I wanted to cry from the pleasure of it, I forced myself to continue as evenly as I could. "Because that's one option we have—one of the *few* we have. We hit the bed, and by the time you completely lose control, I'm ready for you."

That was the option I hoped he chose. Whether

hormones or instincts, I didn't know—but everything inside me was screaming for Erik to carry me over to his giant bed so that we could burn through the curse on his sheets.

Erik groaned again, as if the same thought was crossing his mind—or maybe he imagined just taking me here, with my hands braced against the shelves and his cock thrusting deep into the wetness surrounding his fingers. But even before his rough *"No"* tore from him, I knew what his answer would be.

Despite my raging need, if that was his answer, then I didn't want it this way, either. Not when he couldn't control it. Not when he was forced by the curse. I wanted it to be his choice.

Slowly, his grip eased. His hand slid from between my thighs, the movement dragging the length of his fingers over my throbbing clit. A whimper escaped me.

Erik froze. "Olivia?"

"I'm okay." Dying to feel him inside me, but okay. And as soon as I was out of his arms, the arousal would fade.

But he didn't let me go yet. He set me on my feet, his arm still wrapped around my waist from behind.

I turned my head to look up at him and felt his warm lips brush my temple, a whisper of frigid breath stirring my hair. Just an accidental caress. He'd lowered his head when I'd turned mine. But my heart still drew up tight, because Erik was holding me like a man would hold a woman he cherished.

And I didn't know if he ever would again.

My heart aching, I closed my eyes. "You really think the chimneys are safe?"

A short laugh broke from him. "The Hounds can't fit through them. So, *yes*, little pig—I think they're safe."

I couldn't help but smile. "Are you hungry? You didn't eat anything out there. And I haven't had lunch yet."

"Then I'll feed you." His arm tightened around me. "And we need to talk about…what happens next."

Because he expected me to shoot him. Tears pricking my eyes, I nodded—and finally, he let me go.

It took everything I had not to start crying then.

CHAPTER EIGHT

BY THE TIME WE FINISHED A SIMPLE LUNCH OF sandwiches and soup, the snow still hadn't let up. The Hounds were still out there. So driving away—our one real plan for making it through this—wasn't looking so good.

Erik wasn't either. Feeding me—taking care of me—had seemed to help for a while. But the strain of maintaining control had returned to his expression. His tortured gaze kept settling on my mouth. I knew it wouldn't be long before he started talking about me shooting him again.

This time, I beat him to it.

"I have a new plan," I said.

Seated at the corner of the kitchen island—as

far away from me as he could get and still eat with me—Erik glanced up. His gaze narrowed. "What plan?"

"To get through tonight. I'll go to the room with the strongest door and a lock."

He closed his eyes. "That won't keep me out."

"Just listen, okay?" I waited until he met my gaze before asking again, "Where's the strongest door?"

"Goddammit, Olivia." He raked icy claws through his hair. "My room. The south tower room."

"All right. First I'll lock you outside—in the gatehouse, so even if you get through the front door, the portcullis will keep out the Hounds. While you're out there, you cover yourself in ice to help you keep control. I'm assuming you won't freeze. Will you?"

A reluctant smile tugged at his mouth. "No."

"Good. Then I'll lock myself in your bedroom and wait. So that's two strong doors you'll have to break through to get to me."

"And I *will.*"

"I know, but hear me out. You want me to kill you. I can't do it like this. But if you're busting apart a thick oak door to come get me, if you rip through something that solid, I'm going to be pretty afraid of you. Terrified, actually." I had Erik's attention now. On a deep breath, I said, "If I'm that scared, I'll be able to shoot you."

"In the head. Anywhere else won't stop me."

I nodded. "Right between the eyes."

He held himself rigid, his gaze burning. "Will you truly do it?"

"If you knew how many times I'd seen *The Shining* and the scene with Jack Nicholson and the axe, you wouldn't ask that. That scares the crap out of me every time. But if it helps…" I raised my right hand. "I swear that if you bust through that bedroom door, I'll pull the trigger."

Erik didn't appear convinced. I couldn't blame him; it wasn't much of a plan.

With a sigh, I dropped my hand to my side. "Do you have any better ideas?"

"Aside from you shooting me now?"

"Yes."

"I don't. God, Olivia. I don't want to risk you like this."

His hoarse admission scraped painfully over my heart. "Maybe we'll get lucky," I said softly. "Maybe the curse won't overwhelm your control. Maybe the doors will stop you."

Maybe we'd think of something else.

"Maybe," he agreed, though the hollow sound

of it told me that he held little hope.

I tried to hold on to my own hope and to stop my worry and fear from squirming through. Another distraction would help. We had a plan. If we sat here obsessing over every detail until we put it into motion, that fear would bore giant holes through my confidence.

With a wry smile, he glanced down at his plate. "I should have made something better than sandwiches, since it will be my last meal."

"No." Vehemently, I shook my head. He might have been shooting for humor but there was nothing funny about it. "We'll get through this. Tomorrow morning you'll be making me breakfast."

His eyes narrowed. "I'll make dinner for you."

This wasn't a negotiation, damn it. "Breakfast."

"You know that's not likely."

"I *don't* know that. I'll lock you in the gatehouse. You'll stay in control. And tomorrow morning, I want eggs and bacon. And biscuits. Fluffy ones."

"God damn it, Olivia. You are the most—" With a clench of his jaw, Erik cut himself off and stared at me. I stared back, daring him to finish what he'd been about to say. Daring him to tell me that we wouldn't get through this. Finally, he said, "I'll make dinner."

Which *was* telling me that we wouldn't get through this. But I couldn't accept that. My voice was thick as I whispered, "You'll make both."

His expression softened. "I'll fight it as hard as I can."

Eyes stinging, I nodded.

"But I need to prepare you for disappointment," he said gently. "Because I don't have any bacon."

That surprised a laugh from me. I squeezed the bridge of my nose, pushing back the tears. So, okay. We had a plan.

One I had no intention of following through.

Chest aching, I glanced at Erik and found him watching me. Irises like diamonds. Sharp teeth. Blue skin and icy claws.

Was that all? "What happens when you let the frost giant out? What can I expect?"

"I'll be stronger," he said roughly. "Taller. Bigger."

More like a giant. Jesus. Despite my determination to see us through this, needles of fear and uncertainty began to prick at my confidence. "And you'll be like that when you come for me."

"When I'm inside you." His response was a thick, hungry rasp. "When you come for *me*."

My shocked gaze flew to his. I couldn't speak, but my body answered with a deep pulse of need.

My thighs squeezed together against the sudden, hollow ache.

His jaw clenched. The muscles in his arms bulged as his shoulders hunched and his fists tightened. Losing control. But still trying to hold on.

"I'll be like that when you *shoot* me," he finally gritted out. "And you will."

"I swore. You break down the door. I'll shoot you."

"Good." His throat worked. "God, Olivia. There has to be another way. But I can't think of anything but having you."

"It's okay."

"God damn it, it's not! I should be thinking of how to protect you. Instead I'm ready to spread your legs and—" His teeth clamped together and bit off the rest. A tense moment passed before he continued, "It's not just the physical change that I'm holding back. I'll say…more. Everything I want. Everything I've been imagining since you showed up at my door. So if I'm going to lock myself in the gatehouse, we need to do this soon. Now. I don't think I'll be making dinner."

Already? Panic gripped my chest. I didn't want to let him go out there yet. Anything he wanted to do to me, he could say it. I didn't care what slipped out. We hadn't even had an hour since he'd returned. I'd hoped for at least a little more time with him.

I wasn't going to get it. He was close to the edge. So he was going to the gatehouse, and I was going upstairs to wait...and pray that my instincts were right and he wouldn't hurt me.

But it was more than instinct. I'd seen what lay beneath his control and the need raging inside him. His words exposed what he'd wanted—to be inside me. That wasn't all he'd said, though.

He wanted to make me come. To please me. Not hurt me. But his strength would be so great and his control so thin, he didn't trust himself not to do it.

So I had to trust that he wouldn't.

"All right." I rose from the barstool, but the predatory narrowing of his diamond eyes stopped me. Heart racing, I said, "Maybe you should go out ahead of me."

"Yes."

But Erik didn't move toward the hall. My throat constricted when his gaze touched mine. Despair made an emotional wasteland of his features. God. I could hardly bear the pain there, and the stark desperation in his eyes as he seemed to drink me in. What must be racing through his mind? Believing that he'd die soon…and I'd be the last person he would ever see. But I couldn't read more beneath his desolate expression. Was he regretting that he'd ever laid eyes on me? Wondering how the hell someone like me had been the source of his destruction?

I wouldn't be. I yearned to tell him that we'd be fine, that we'd get through this night.

But I couldn't. It might all go horribly wrong, and this might be the last time I saw him without being terrified or forced into an action that I desperately wanted to avoid. So instead of reassuring him that we'd be okay, I only returned his gaze while fighting back tears.

"Erik." I could barely speak. "Is there anything you want me to tell anyone?"

"No. Everyone else who matters knows how I feel. And you should know how much I…that I—" His eyes closed for a long second. When he opened them, determination had replaced the desolation, but it still lingered in the rasp of his voice. "You should know that I wouldn't burden you with this. If I could help it. If my father hadn't fucked everything up."

"I know," I whispered.

"But I swear to you, Olivia. I swear that if you miss the shot, or if you can't pull the trigger…if

I have any control at all, I'll do everything in my power not to hurt you."

"I believe it." My plan rode on that belief.

"But don't miss," he warned harshly.

"I won't."

As if searching for the truth, his tormented gaze held mine for another long moment. He abruptly pivoted and strode to the hall. My heart dropped at the sudden movement, then I was on my feet, following him—marveling at his strength. Erik believed that he walked to his death, yet his shoulders were set in an unyielding line that seemed broad enough to support the world. No hesitation slowed his long strides. He'd made his choice; now he was determined to follow it through.

He'd made his choice…and he didn't know that I'd already made another for him.

Doubts crowded my mind again. Was I doing the right thing? What if his decision hadn't stemmed just from a desire to protect me, but because he'd rather die than be with someone the curse had forced on him?

In the gatehouse, Erik faced me again, his eyes a sharp diamond. Immediately, a thick pillar of ice began climbing his legs, completely encasing their strong lengths. It rose to his stomach. His chest.

With emotion clogging my throat, I halted in the doorway, watching the ice engulf his body. Uncertainty held me in its rough grip. My insides felt as if they'd been worked over by coarse sandpaper, and I had to know— "Erik!"

My panicked cry halted the ice's advance. Glacial blue surrounded him up to his chest. In that solid block, I'd have felt trapped and cold, and utterly alone. He only watched me, waiting. Frost glittered in his blue-black hair.

I swallowed hard. "When I asked you out to dinner a few months ago…if not for the curse, would you have said yes? Would you have ever wanted to be with me?"

"It doesn't matter. I can't be."

Maybe he could for one night. I just needed to know if he'd ever wanted to. "It matters to me."

"All right. I wouldn't have said yes."

Pain stabbed through my chest. I shouldn't have asked. Because if that was his answer, I hadn't really wanted to know.

"Oh," I whispered.

"But only because you wouldn't have needed to ask me," he added softly. "If not for the curse, I wouldn't have stopped kissing you the first time."

My heart jumped. He wouldn't have *stopped*?

"I thought you only kissed me because of the curse."

"No." His gaze burned into mine. "I walked away because of the curse. I kissed you because I wanted to."

The ice began rising again as he spoke. Up to his shoulders. His neck. Trembling, I wanted to shout at him to stop, not to go any farther. I wanted to close my eyes so I wouldn't have to watch. I wanted to cry.

I didn't let myself do any of that. "A kiss wasn't worth your life, Erik."

"Yes, it was." His brief smile appeared before fading into bleak regret. "But it wasn't worth risking yours. So I wish I never had—and that I'd never met you."

My throat closed. I knew he meant that I would've been safer if we hadn't met. It didn't matter. Those words still hurt.

And even knowing the danger, I couldn't say the same. I would never be sorry that I'd met him. That I'd kissed him.

I was only sorry that I hadn't realized it before these past few days.

He never looked away as the ice covered him completely, then began filling the gatehouse. And even though I couldn't see the future, I knew that if it all went wrong tonight, Erik Gulbrandr would haunt me for the rest of my life.

CHAPTER NINE

FOR NEARLY TWO DAYS, I'D WAITED AND WORRIED myself almost to madness, not knowing where Erik was or how he was doing. Now I knew exactly where he was, but the waiting was so much worse. I couldn't sit still. Even pretending to read was impossible. At one point, I forced myself into bed, telling myself that I should rest a little. The astronomical solstice would come just after one o'clock; I'd be exhausted by then and less capable of dealing with whatever happened. If Erik broke through the front door, the noise would surely wake me. But instead of napping, I just lay in his giant bed and stared up at the darkened ceiling, so alert that even the faint creak of the heavy snow settling on the roof sent my heart jolting against my ribs.

The futility of sleep had me throwing back the covers and moving to the window. The storm had finally let up. Moonlight bathed the clearing in front of the house, a bright silvery glow against the white.

Movement near the treeline caught my eye. A wolf. Not one of the big ones—not a Hound. Its yellow eyes gleamed through the darkness. Looking up at me. I had the sudden, eerie certainty that the Hound watched the house through the animal. Making sure that Erik and I didn't make a run for it? Or just waiting for him to lose control so that they could attack while his guard was down?

Maybe both reasons. With a shiver, I scanned the shadows between the trees. Nothing. If the two Hounds were converging on the house, they weren't bold enough to show themselves yet.

The muscles in the back of my neck tensed. The gray wolf had begun to slink across the snow toward the gatehouse. It sniffed around the stone before peering through the portcullis. From this angle, I couldn't see Erik or the ice that surrounded him, but he must have known the wolf was there. An explosion of snow suddenly erupted beneath the animal's nose. With a yelp, the wolf scurried back to the edge of the trees, tail between its legs.

I grinned—then caught my breath in realization. The moon was out. The storm was over. And Erik could clear the roads. I could make it to the highway.

But was it too late for me to drive far enough? And there were still two Hounds out there, not just one. Erik and I might be able to draw them out, but they weren't stupid. It would only take one trick, one distraction, and while one Hound kept Erik occupied, the other could come after me. Then I had no doubt they'd use me against Erik. They'd already tried.

Or at least one brother had tried. Erik had said the Hounds didn't work well together. But maybe they didn't need to. The gray wolves could be a distraction or a threat, too.

A distraction. Such as waiting until both Erik and I were paying attention to the wolf at the edge of the clearing? For what purpose? The house was solid. The ice around Erik was solid. The brothers couldn't get to either of us.

But now I was uneasy. Holding my breath, I listened. Just the crackle of the fire. Yet my instincts were screaming.

Heart pounding, I scrambled across the bed. My pistol lay on the nightstand. Erik expected me to shoot him with it. I'd much rather shoot the Hounds. Sitting motionless on the wide mattress with my gun in hand, I faced the open door and the dark hallway that led to the northern tower room.

Still no sound except the fire. Even the creaking roof was quiet now. *Okay.* So maybe I was freaking myself out for nothing. How could a Hound get in? The windows were barred; even if they managed to break through, I'd have heard them. Erik had told me about the bolt-hole in the pantry that led to an escape tunnel, but that had been reinforced as well as the rest of the house. The Hounds might have found the tunnel entrance, but they couldn't get into it.

The chimney?

I'd only asked myself so that I could laugh about it and ease this horrible tension. Erik had said the Hounds were too big. I believed that. And yet...and yet...the roof had been creaking. I couldn't remember it doing so before—and it wasn't creaking now.

And if the Hounds had a wolf watching the place, they might have had a wolf listening, too. Maybe my stupid little joke to Erik had *told* the brothers how to get in.

I glanced to the fireplace. I'd have noticed if

something had been making its way through the chimney shaft. Soot scraped from inside would have fallen in. Probably some snow, too.

But the fireplace in the other tower room? Or the great room downstairs?

Trembling with anxiety, I watched the shadows in the hallway. Nothing moved. I was just scaring myself. The dark probably wasn't helping. On a deep, calming breath, I placed the weapon on the nightstand and flicked on the lamp, revealing the gigantic snake slithering silently down the hallway, lidless eyes glinting yellow and thick muscles undulating beneath silver scales.

Horror strangled the breath from my lungs. That couldn't be real. Though the Hounds could shape-shift, Erik had only mentioned them transforming into wolves and humans. It had to be another trick, an illusion, but all at once I recalled the Ironwood witch's other children—including a serpent big enough to circle the world.

Oh, my God. I dived for the gun.

"Erik!" My scream rose into a shriek as the snake moved in my peripheral vision, no longer slinking its way toward the bedroom but coiling its long body as if preparing to rear up and strike. *"Erik!"*

A noise thundered from below, as if a tank had rammed through the stone wall. He wouldn't be fast enough. I spun around, bracing my shoulders against the backboard, aiming between my knees. God, god. The snake was already inside the bedchamber. It was too fast; I couldn't track it in my sights. The broad, flat head whipped from side to side, offering only a narrow, moving target. Its jaw unhinged, six-inch fangs unfolding like switchblades, and I remembered reading how Thor, a freaking *god*, had been killed by the Midgard serpent's poison. After destroying the beast, he'd taken nine steps and fallen dead. If that shit got into my blood, I wouldn't last a second.

Screw the head. I'd settle for hurting it a little.

I fired. The gun kicked against my grip, the crack deafening in the stone chamber. *Missed.* I didn't have time for despair. Screaming, I squeezed off another shot. Another. The next ripped through its neck, but satisfaction was a fleeting thing, because it was at the side of the bed now, rising up like a cobra, and this was it, I was dead.

Fuck giving in, though. I aimed at the gaping fanged maw and fired.

At nothing.

Ears ringing painfully, I stared at the empty

space. Another illusion? No.

Erik.

I hadn't seen him or heard him come in. But he must have grabbed the snake's tail and yanked it away from me just in time. It lay halfway across the chamber. A spear impaled its midsection, pinning it to the stone floor. His beautiful face a mask of fury, Erik approached the thrashing head.

"Watch the fangs!" I cried out. The ringing in my ears muffled the warning, and it was as if Erik didn't hear it, either.

The snake struck. I screamed as its long fangs sank through Erik's jeans, stabbing deep into his thigh. He barely reacted, simply clenching his teeth and reaching down to grip the snake's jaws, wedging his fingers into its mouth.

In a single sharp movement, he ripped the serpent's head and throat in half as easily as I would tear apart a length of string cheese. Blood spewed over his hands, his leg. The smell hit me, hot and coppery. My stomach heaved. I dropped the gun and covered my mouth, staring at him over the tips of my fingers. My vision blurred as the full terror of everything that had just happened rolled over me—and the devastation of what was to come.

"The poison, Erik," I whispered. "Oh, my God,

the poison."

He let go of the snake's jaws and the two halves of its head flopped to the floor. His lips moved, but through the ringing in my ears his response sounded as if it came from miles away. "I've already healed."

Of course. Nothing could kill him but a bullet to the head or the Hounds ripping out his throat. But for a moment, I'd been certain that I'd lose him, and it was as if everything inside me had been torn apart. But he was still here. Alive. I stared at him, my breath coming in ragged sobs.

His diamond gaze searched my face. "You're all right?"

No. No, I wasn't. But I couldn't say it, because the concern in Erik's expression transformed into torment even as he looked at me. Averting his face, he stared at his bloodied hands before slowly clenching them to fists at his sides. Close to the edge of his control…and probably worried that he might be tipping over.

I nodded—*I'm just fine,* that gesture lied—but my sobbing breaths probably told him the truth, anyway.

The bleak edge to his voice penetrated the hollow ringing in my head. "You aren't safe here.

Even if you stop me, the last Hound can get in."

My heart twisted. That wasn't just the torment I saw in him now, but desolation. Because the one thing he'd relied on—the house keeping me safe after he was gone—couldn't do that anymore.

I scooted to the end of the bed, then froze when his burning gaze snapped to mine, then slowly slid down my body. By the time our eyes met again, his erection was straining against denim. The curse was gaining traction again.

God. I wanted him. I would welcome him into my bed. But I preferred that it wasn't while he was covered in a snake's blood and my skin was still slick with cold sweat. "So what now?"

"The first plan." Determination hardened his face. "We drive out of here. When the Hound comes for us, I stop him and you keep going."

My gaze shot to the window. Already dark. The astronomical solstice was less than four hours away. "Can I get far enough?"

His throat worked before he answered, "Maybe. If you don't, promise me the same as you did before. If I catch up to you, if I rip off the door, you have to shoot me."

Because I might be out in the middle of nowhere. Because he might drag me out of the truck and into the snow—and because he believed wouldn't be able to stop fucking long enough to keep me from freezing to death. But would I rather take my chances with Erik and trust that he'd take more care than that, or face another snake?

I glanced at the bloodied monster on the floor. The answer was pretty simple, actually. "All right," I said softly, not moving yet. "I need to get off the bed and get dressed. So don't jump me, okay? I'm not running away."

Jaw clenched, Erik nodded. When he looked at me, the ravenous need in his eyes stole my breath. "Hurry," he rasped.

I hurried.

EVERYTHING OUTSIDE WAS QUIET. ABSOLUTELY still. If the Hound or the wolves were nearby, they didn't show themselves as Erik and I rounded the side of the house, where his big truck sat protected under a shield of ice and buried under drifts of snow. As we approached, the snow and ice parted like a frozen Red Sea, revealing gleaming chrome and red paint.

"Show off," I said.

The fierce look he'd been directing toward the treeline abruptly changed to a grin. My heart tripped. God. Did he have any idea how incredible he was? So what if he was tall and strong and gorgeous. None of that mattered compared to the way he stood before me, spear at his side and valiantly fighting against a thousand-year-old curse in a desperate attempt to protect me. A warrior. *My* warrior, at least for tonight.

His gaze searched my face. "Promise me, Olivia—no matter what happens when the Hound comes, you'll drive on."

My throat tightened. "I will. Now bend down a little."

Though his eyebrows drew together, he did. I dropped my bag on the snow beside my feet. Grasping his collar, I rose up onto the toes of my boots. The snow helped—heavier, he sank deeper into it than I did, so I didn't have to go up so far.

When I felt his frigid breath against my lips, I whispered, "Control yourself, or the Hound will get us. This is for luck."

Erik didn't move, didn't respond. He probably didn't dare.

I knew better than to do more than softly press my mouth to his. Feverish, his firm lips burned against mine, and I savored the heat and contact as long as I could. Not long enough.

It never could be.

His hand came up to cup my jaw as I sank back onto my heels. Tipped by an icy claw, his broad thumb stroked my bottom lip.

"For luck," he said roughly.

I nodded and drew a long breath. "All right." I reached for my bag. "Let's ride like the wind."

All at once the warrior again, Erik scanned the trees as I started the engine and began blasting the heater. As soon as I nodded through the window at him, he leapt easily into the truck bed and thumped the roof of the cab twice.

Time to roll. The bright halogen headlights illuminated the clearing, replacing gentle moonlight with harsh white. Like a cloth seam splitting and revealing skin below, the snow cleared from the driveway ahead of us. Erik had told me to go fast, so I made the tires spit gravel. My hands tight on the steering wheel, my heart pounding, I barely slowed around the corners. We flew past the trees lining the drive, their trunks dark against all that ghostly white, and every second I expected the Hound to jump out from between them.

We reached the road. The remains of my Jeep had all but disappeared beneath a mound of snow. No plows had come this way yet, at least not for the past day or so. The county didn't need to send one now. Within a blink, Erik cleared the pavement. I eased out onto the blacktop, expecting ice. The road was dry.

I gunned the engine. Only a few miles to the main highway—and only a few miles more until the highway ran along a narrow gorge, with a river on one side and sheer cliffs on the other. If the Hound followed us, he'd have to pass through that bottleneck. Erik intended to wait there for him while I drove on.

If the Hound didn't attack us first.

Tension had a stiff hold on my every muscle. My fingers were already aching thanks to my death grip on the steering wheel. My only job was to focus on the road—Erik would watch for the Hound. Despite that, my gaze still darted from side to side, searching the tall snowbanks, flicking into the trees.

A wolf burst out of the snow and dashed across the road. I'd prepared myself for every trick and illusion that I could imagine. Before we'd left, I'd decided that no matter what showed up in front of me—Hound, wolf, or little old lady—I'd run them over with Erik's big truck. Just ram right into them.

Reflexes took over and I slammed the brake, instead. The tires screeched. I jolted forward against the seatbelt, then my head overrode reflex and I hit the gas.

And rammed into the Hound.

Screaming, I stomped the brake again. The Hound's body flew thirty feet before smashing into the pavement. Horror shattered through me—*I'd just killed a man*—but he was already rising to his feet, his silvery hair gleaming white in the bright headlights.

The same Hound who'd threatened us on the first day. The same one who'd sniffed my panties. I barely had a second to recognize him before he shape-shifted, then guilty horror became sheer terror.

I'd seen them as giant wolves before, but even though they'd been huge, they'd *looked* like wolves. This Hound transformed into something in-between, an unnatural nightmare that stood on hind legs.

A *werewolf*, my petrified mind supplied, but nothing I'd ever watched on a movie screen resembled the grotesque monster the Hound had become. The transition had been smooth—no bones popping or claws ripping through fingertips—but the result was a twisted mash of human and wolf and *wrong*. Long, thin arms lightly covered in hair hung past powerful furred haunches and lupine knees. The hands were enormous, the fingers bending on an extra joint and armed with razored claws. But the face was the worst, still bald as a man's but shaped like a wolf's, pale skin and pink lips stretched over a pointed muzzle and gaping open to reveal a predator's teeth.

The better to rip out Erik's throat, my dear.

Already shaking, I jumped in my seat when Erik vaulted over the roof of the cab and crouched in front of the truck, spear at his side. For an instant, frost giant and Hound stared each other down. The werewolf snarled, slobbering human lips drawing back over its fangs. I couldn't see Erik's expression, only read the tension in his broad back, in the sinews of his forearms, his muscles like chiseled stone.

Suddenly chunks of ice exploded from the snowbanks ahead, pelting the Hound. None of the chunks were big or sharp enough to hurt it, but that wasn't Erik's intention, I realized. He'd just wanted the distraction.

He hurled the spear—then charged after it. Batting away the flying chunks of ice, the Hound focused on Erik again. Too late. The spear stabbed through its furred chest, knocking him back a step, then Erik was on him. The Hound's head jerked to the side, avoiding Erik's grip; Erik got his hands on the creature's shoulder, instead. In a shower of blood, the werewolf's long thin arm went flying.

An agonized howl pierced the quiet. I watched, too stunned to even reach for my gun as a new arm began growing. It was all happening so fast, I could barely track it. Erik had gripped the spear again, was forcing the shaft up through the werewolf's ribcage. The Hound slashed at him, claws ripping open Erik's side. Crimson splattered over snow.

My hands and clenched teeth stopped my scream. That wound would heal within seconds and I couldn't distract Erik now—he might think I was in trouble here.

And why wasn't I? Sickened, terrified, I wildly looked away from the battle, searching for the wolves. There'd been at least one a few seconds ago. Now I feared they'd sneak up behind Erik while he was fighting the Hound or attack the truck, but not even a single wolf was in sight.

I glanced back. I hadn't looked away for more than two seconds, but the fight was over.

Trembling hands covering my mouth, I stared. That horrible human-wolf head was just a bloody pulp with a mane of silver hair. Erik yanked his spear from the Hound's ravaged chest and threw the body to the side of the road, where the snow-bank seemed to swallow it up.

Slowly, he turned toward the truck. I was supposed to have been driving on. I hadn't realized the whole battle would only last ten seconds. Heart thundering, I rolled down the window as he approached, ripping the blood-soaked shirt from his torso.

Oh, God. Not in the snow. *Not in the snow.* But I didn't reach for the gun.

He passed the brilliant wash of the headlights and his own eyes shone in the dark, a pale blue glow. His big hands gripped the edge of the driver's side door, fingers tipped with shards of ice.

"Olivia." My name rumbled from him, rough and low. "You're all right?"

"Yes," I whispered. He was, too. The gash on his side had already healed, leaving nothing but blue skin and taut muscle. "What about the body?"

"Odin's ravens will come for it at dawn. You just need to get the hell out of here." His jaw like granite, he stepped back. "Are you heading east or west?"

"East."

"So I'll go west for as long as I can."

My breath shuddering, my throat a solid ache, I

nodded. "I want fluffy biscuits tomorrow morning," I said hoarsely. "Don't forget."

The anguish bleeding through his faint smile seemed to mirror the agony inside me, but though I could hardly bear to see his, Erik didn't look away from my face. "I'll try, Olivia."

I knew he would. But I couldn't respond—he was already gone. Heading west as fast as he could.

Wiping the tears from my cheeks, I rolled up the window. Carefully I drove past the splatters of blood that were all that was left of the Hound. And there was a wolf, lying dead against the snowbank. Erik hadn't covered it with snow—maybe because a dead wolf wouldn't raise as many questions as the Hound's body would. I slowed, looking at it. That was the spot where the Hound's arm had landed, too. I didn't see the thin limb now. Just that wolf. It must have attacked Erik when I'd looked away. Everything had happened so fast.

But I wasn't going fast enough now. I didn't know if I *could* go fast enough. But there was one way to find out—and now that I was on the road, I should have cell reception again.

Even as I reached into my bag for my phone, it rang. Of course it did.

"Hi, Mom," I answered, my voice breaking with

sheer relief when she returned my greeting. "If I keep driving, is Erik going to catch up with me?"

"Yes."

My heart stopped. I stared through the windshield. The highway was coming up. So what now? Stop somewhere and just wait for him? Try to get a hotel room? But it was the holidays and ski season; I probably couldn't find a room anywhere along this corridor.

Would he catch me in the truck? "Am I going to be okay?"

But even as the question left my mouth, I realized how stupid it was. Of course I'd be okay. If my mother had seen a future in which I wasn't going to make it through this, if I was injured or hadn't consented, then she and my dad would be here already—or she'd tell me to pull over and take aim as soon as I saw Erik coming.

Her heavy sigh sounded through the speaker. "I don't know what to tell you, Liv."

I blinked. That wasn't the answer I'd expected. What couldn't she tell me? There were only two choices: Yes, I'd be hurt; or no, I wouldn't.

But hurt wasn't always physical—and Mom never protected my sister and me from our own hearts.

"It's okay." I'd deal with the emotional stuff when the time came. Until then, there were more important things to worry about, such as not getting fucked by a frost giant in the cab of a truck. Erik would take me wherever he found me, and the dimensions of the front seat weren't exactly ideal. The Gulbrandrs' fortress was close, but the remains of the giant snake were still splattered through the tower room. "Can I make it home?"

She paused before answering. This time, she wasn't looking ahead at a future lying on a course that was already plotted. Instead she was feeling out alternatives, which was harder for her.

Finally she said, "Drive fast."

I hung up the phone and drove.

Chapter Ten

I reached Denver just before eleven. Two hours still remained before the solstice. Not much time, and my gut was screaming that Erik wasn't far behind me. I sped through the snowy streets as fast as I dared. Never had I been so grateful for my job and the contacts I'd made in real estate and development, because when I'd decided to move out of my apartment a few years ago, I'd called in a few favors and gotten dibs on a property that was as isolated as one could get in the city without spending a fortune. My house sat alone on a dead end street near a nature preserve at the south end of the city. There was nothing behind my place but a few trails, deserted at this time of night. And I had a pretty good arm, but I couldn't throw a stone and hit the nearest house.

Erik had said he'd tear apart mountains to get to me. That was fine. I just didn't want him to tear apart my neighbors. Luckily, mine didn't live too close.

The house was freezing. I clicked on the heat and rushed to my bedroom, tearing away my coat and sweater as I went. With skin prickled and shivering, I moved to the French doors that opened my room to the deck overlooking the preserve. The full moon shone above. Beyond the back yard, there was nothing but snow and trees, but I didn't know which door he'd use to enter the house…if he used a door at all. My house might have a gaping hole in the wall within a few hours.

I looked to my bed. Blankets—I needed more blankets. Over my comforter I spread a quilt and an unzipped sleeping bag. Ugly, but I didn't think Erik would notice or care. With the heater cranked up, the wooden floor had lost its chill on my bare feet by the time I finished, and I stripped down to my panties and a tank. I considered waiting naked— making my consent as obvious as possible, no matter the state Erik was in. But if everything went horribly wrong, I didn't want to be nude.

Hoping that this night would go right, I placed a box of condoms on the nightstand near my bed. Preparing for the worst, I hid my gun in the nightstand drawer.

Now I only needed to prepare myself.

I turned off the lights and crawled beneath the top quilt, pushing my hand into my panties. Erik had said he wouldn't be able to slow down long enough to prepare me, so I pictured it now: his tongue slipping through the wet and warmth, his fingers tugging at my nipples. Falling into this daydream was easy; in the past year and a half, I'd been here so many times, imagining him with me.

Soon he would be. I closed my eyes, letting go of doubts and fear, remembering his hardness behind me, the taste of his kiss, the heat of his skin. Remembering the gentle, devastating glide of his fingers over my clitoris.

Biting my lip against a moan, I mimicked the same touch. I was already as drenched as I'd been then.

You're in need, Olivia.

So much. Though desperate to rub harder, faster, I only teased, imagining each light touch was a flick of Erik's tongue. God. *God.* Even going slow, this fantasy was going to make me come.

Too early. Better to keep myself primed. Groaning, I pulled my hand away, thighs squeezing together, my flesh empty and aching. I stared up at the ceiling and tried not to picture Erik's head between my legs.

The room abruptly dimmed, as if the moon passed behind a cloud. I glanced at the French doors and gooseflesh rose over my skin. Frost climbed the panes in a thick, crystalline layer. Though the opaque glass, the full moon outside was nothing but a diffused glow. My breath steamed in front of me, each pant visible in puffs.

He was here.

Pulse suddenly racing, I clutched the blanket to my chest and shot a look at the door leading to the darkened hallway. I hadn't lied when I'd said that if he'd broke through solid wood, I'd be terrified. Maybe scared enough to shoot him.

So I'd left every door in my house open. Inviting him in before inviting him inside me—and it wasn't fear that gripped me now, but anticipation and hope. Until this moment, my whole being had been focused on getting through this night. But I didn't just want this night. I wanted more from him. Erik called himself mostly a man, but he was everything that I wanted in a man. If there was more to him....I would soon see what that was, too.

Waiting, I stared into the dark, intensely aware of the hardness of my nipples beneath the soft cotton of my tank. I didn't know if it was in reaction to the cold or the arousal blooming through me, but the sensation deepened the needy ache between my thighs.

Shadows moved in the hall. Abruptly Erik filled the entrance to my room—bigger and taller than he'd been only a few hours before, his head almost even with the top of the door frame. My breath stopped as the diffused moonlight struck his muscled form. His *naked* form. Not blue now, his skin was as pale as sculpted marble, but there'd never been a statue so perfectly made. His broad shoulders narrowed to a ridged abdomen. Dark hair led a trail to his groin. His rigid penis jutted from between powerful thighs.

Oh...my *God.* The condoms weren't part of the plan anymore. If I'd been prepared properly, I'd have bought the larger size. The giant size.

But it was okay. I wouldn't panic. I was on birth control. I'd just pray that 'frost giant' wasn't a STD— and that he wouldn't rip me in half. Because I'd been with my share of guys, but none of them had been swinging around anything like *that.*

"Olivia."

His deep voice was the low thunder of a cracking glacier. His hands gripped the sides of the door frame, his arms straining. Muscle and sinew stood in sharp relief.

Still holding himself back, somehow—even though the power of the curse was almost at its height.

"It's all right, Erik." I needed to ease his mind about this, if nothing else. "I want you. I want this."

Wood splintered beneath his hands. The door frame cracked as he came through, as if he'd forced his way inside instead of trying to stop himself. His eyes glittered like diamond chips in a hot blue flame.

I tossed back the quilt to welcome him in.

He didn't come around the bed, as I expected. Long strides carried him on a straight line to me, up over the foot of the mattress. With a sweep of his arm, he tore the bedcover completely away, baring my legs. Big hands circled my ankles. I cried out when he suddenly dragged me toward him. My back hit the sleeping bag spread out beneath me, my tank sliding up to expose my stomach and friction a soft burn against my skin as he pulled me closer. Then he was pushing my legs apart, his big body rising over mine.

My breath came in sharp pants. My brain struggled to catch up. He'd said he wouldn't be able to prepare me. I still hadn't expected this so fast. But he was truly just going to fuck me.

Claws slipped under my panties and pulled; my hips jerked upward, lace biting into my skin before ripping free. His breath was ice on my face, his body a heavy furnace above me.

Powerful thighs spread mine wider. He braced his hands beside my shoulders, his glittering eyes locked on mine. Hot and blunt, the head of his cock wedged against my entrance.

Holding on to him, my fingernails dug into the steely muscles of his biceps, my mind racing. This was going to happen, it was happening *now*—

He surged forward. I was wet and aroused, but nothing could have prepared me for his size. So big and deep. My lips parted on a shocked cry, cut short as his cock drove into me again. I gasped for a breath and already he was pushing inside me again, filling me, each thrust strong and deep. Not pounding into me, there was no pain, I was just full, *so* full, and each stroke seemed to strike sparks across every nerve within the sensitive flesh stretched tight around his big invading shaft. All at once an orgasm ripped through me, shock and pleasure and heat rolled up into an avalanche of sensation, my inner muscles rippling around his thick cock and he didn't stop, but fucked me relentlessly as I came, writhing uncontrollably beneath him.

And he still fucked me as the orgasm receded, leaving me wetter than I'd ever been. My body suddenly felt boneless, my legs falling wide. The tension gone, the incredible sensation of Erik inside me was utter decadence. My back rose in a languid arch, relishing the steady rise and fall of his powerful form, of his thick penis driving into me in long, endless thrusts.

I needed to touch him. My palms slid over heavy muscle, fevered skin. Above me, Erik was rigid and shaking, even as he rocked deep into me. His head was bowed, his teeth clenched, and his features a mask of desolation and defeat.

"Hurting...you." Each broken word sounded like an anguished echo from the pit of Hell.

Didn't he know? Had he mistaken my shock for pain? Maybe even my orgasm seemed like the writhing of a woman in agony, and he'd only seen what he'd expected to see. I caught his face between my hands.

"You're not hurting me, Erik," I said softly, holding his tormented gaze even as my body welcomed each heavy thrust. "*Feel* me. Feel how good it is, how wet I am."

I linked my legs around his hips, holding him close and rising to meet every surge of his body into mine. Slowly his torment seemed to fade, though each thrust was just as hard, his muscles just as rigid, his rhythm just as relentless. My own languid ease was slipping away, my body tightening with need. The tension renewed, each stroke left me breathless.

"See?" Panting, I couldn't manage more. "Not hurting. You feel…amazing."

"*Olivia.*"

His voice was still rough, as if simply speaking was another battle against the curse—but no longer anguished. Just hungry.

God, so was I. Starving for his touch, for him to give me more than his cock, but the curse forced him to fuck me and I didn't know if he could offer any more while in its grip. It didn't matter. I had a lot of practice imagining that my fingers were his.

Back arching, I cupped my breasts. My nipples were tight and the sweep of my thumbs a delicious tease. But not only for me.

Erik's eyes flared white-hot as he glanced between us. My gaze locked on his face, I pinched the throbbing tips and his ravenous groan was the sweetest reward.

With pleasure trembling through me, I pinched them again, right to the edge of pain, so that every sensation sharpened. The thrust of his cock into me. The feverish heat of his skin. The chill of the air upon my sweat-slicked flesh. I moaned his name and his stiffened arms beside me suddenly flexed, elbows bending as he lowered his head.

Cold breath whispered over my breast. For a bright, frozen moment I remembered the sharpness of his teeth, then his cold tongue slicked a path around my nipple and the icy shock of it tightened every inch of my skin. I cried out, my back arching higher, my hips tilting to take him deeper, and he was fucking me just right, just right, my flesh a taut shiver beneath the coldness of his mouth and my pussy clenching around his thick shaft, coming hard and harder and still he fucked me, thrusting deep, his cock feeling even bigger inside me or I just couldn't feel anything else.

Tears streaked my face as I came down, shaking and spent but the exquisite ache already building again with every thrust.

With a groan, Erik lifted his head. His thumb brushed my cheek. Wiping away the tears.

Torment filled his voice again. "*No.*"

I caught his hand, shaking my head, wrapping my legs tighter around him. "It's not pain, Erik. I've just never come that hard before."

His growled response held a note of possessive satisfaction. A short laugh escaped me, then I bit my lip on a moan as his next thrust was deeper, harder. God.

"Lift me up a little," I told him breathlessly. "Help me take you."

His hand wedged under the small of my back, angling my hips up and relieving the heavy weight between my thighs. He was fucking up into me now, not just fucking me into the bed, and the new angle was perfect. My fingers slipped between us, gliding over my clit. I was so wet, my slick arousal painting my inner thighs and glistening over his cock, and soon I was writhing and crying out again, because it was too much, too much, but even when I pulled my hand away he didn't stop, just fucking me, making me come until I had nothing left and my entire body was languid again.

Then I simply clung to him, loving the sensation of him moving inside me. I didn't know how long I held on to him. Minutes. Hours. Forever. Not long enough. I closed my eyes, and then I was lost again, lost to the surge of him, the endless need that wrung everything from me, crying his name until my voice gave out, exhaustion a heavy weight on my flesh, my mind a fog of pleasure that only cleared briefly as Erik suddenly stiffened with his cock wedged deep. He shuddered and I gasped as the frigid pulse of his seed filled my heated sheath.

Then he rolled onto his side, his arms wrapping around me and pulling me close. Despite his orgasm, his cock was a hot steel length against my thigh. His body was a solid furnace, and the bedroom air icy cold. But even if the doors were closed and the heater blasting, I knew that I would be far colder when he let go.

How long had it been? I couldn't make the effort to look at the clock. I didn't want to move from his embrace. "Is it over?"

His rough reply followed me into sleep. *"No."*

HOT FINGERS WERE LIFTING ME, sliding a pillow beneath my hips. I stirred, my mind heavy and slow. I lay on my stomach, head cradled in my crossed arms. And Erik was—

Behind me. Positioning me, his hands pushing my thighs apart, tilting my ass higher.

Preparing me.

I jolted fully awake, then gasped out a strangled cry as ice slicked through the folds of my sex.
Licking me. My fingers curled into the blankets
beneath me. My hips bucked against the pillow and
then against the grip of his big hands as he caught
me and held me still for the thrust of his tongue.

"Erik!" I cried out. Then "Oh my god. Oh my
god."

Icy and slick, he delved deeper and found my
clit, soothing my tender flesh, inflaming me all over
again. I screamed, but this time he didn't stiffen
and shake, tormented by worry. Instead it was if he
knew exactly what he was doing to me when his
cold tongue lashed my clitoris, then was followed
by the caress of his broad thumb, his skin burning
with curse's fever. Hot and cold, slick and rough.

Shuddering with desire, I couldn't keep up
with the sensations coursing through me, couldn't
think, could only cry his name as the ecstasy over-
whelmed me, and he growled his pleasure against
my convulsing flesh as I came.

He licked until the orgasm released me and
I collapsed against the pillow, still trembling. The
mattress shifted as he rose between my legs. His
hands gripped my hips and I moaned in desperate
anticipation as he pulled me up to my knees, my

face still cushioned on my folded arms. His body covered mine, heated lips pressing a kiss to my shoulder.

"*Olivia.*" Another kiss burned my nape. "*You taste so good.*"

A shiver ripped through me when he licked the spot he'd kissed, then the blunt pressure of his cock lodged at my entrance. Last time he'd simply taken me. Not this time.

"*More?*"

"Yes." Moaning my answer, I spread my knees wider. "Yes."

For a long moment, there was only the harsh sound of his breathing behind me. Then an icy claw skimmed down my spine, not painful, only unexpected, but even as my body tightened with surprise his cock pushed deep inside me. *Oh, my God.* He'd felt big before but the sensation of his thick shaft pushing past the clenching resistance of my inner muscles detonated within me, ecstasy colliding with frenzied need. I cried out as he withdrew slightly, my hips thrusting back against him, trying to force him deeper. He caught my waist, one hand sliding around to cup my breast. Ice slipped over my nipple and he slammed into me, a harsh groan ripping from his chest as my pussy clamped down on his cock again.

With a strangled moan, I pushed back against him. I was losing myself again, until there nothing but desire and the feel of him inside me. He was supposed to be the one with no control, yet here I was, utterly helpless to this need. No curse necessary—or maybe love was the same thing.

Then ice scraped over my clit, he shoved deep, and I was gone.

"Olivia?"

Erik. My eyelids were too heavy to lift, my throat raw, so I only sighed. He was so warm. Naked. Pulling me closer.

"Tell me you're all right, Olivia."

I couldn't ignore the concern in his voice. "Mmm-hmmm. Just sleepy."

"Thank God." His arms tightened around me. His chest hitched against my back. "I used you so hard."

"Yeah." Yawning, I turned in his embrace and kissed the hollow of his throat before lazily winding my arms around his neck. My fingers tangled in his short hair. "It was nice."

This was, too. Lying against him with a mound

of blankets pulled over us—he must have done that. Or maybe I did. The past few hours were pretty hazy. The last thing I remembered for certain was coming my brains out.

Now the curse no longer had a hold on him... yet he was still holding *me*. All at once, everything that I'd told myself not to hope for came rushing back.

I slitted my eyes open and my heart stopped. In the gray, pre-dawn light, Erik was gazing down at me, and I recognized the agonized need in his eyes. I'd probably looked at him like that all night.

"Erik," I whispered, then his mouth was on mine, sweet and warm. No fever. No ice. But there was still hunger.

Moaning, I parted my lips and welcomed the thrust of his tongue, my heart blooming with a wonderful, unbearable ache. For so long, I'd held onto the memory of a single moment, when he'd kissed me as if he needed me. As if he already loved me. A kiss that told me he was the one.

With a tortured groan, Erik swept his hand down my body, hooking my thigh over his hip. "One more, Olivia." Lifting his head, he spoke the hoarse plea against my swollen lips. "One more. God, please. Let me have this once and I swear I'll never touch you again."

I didn't want him to swear that. But I only had time to nod before his mouth captured mine again, stealing the rest of my response and my heart was full, so full, because Erik was kissing me as if he never wanted to let me go.

Just as he'd kissed me before.

ERIK WAS GONE WHEN I woke. His absence wasn't too surprising. The clock told me that it was past noon. Sunlight streamed through the windows. I couldn't imagine him lying around when there were things to be done.

I wasn't sorry that he wouldn't see me roll over and groan as the full effect of last night hit me. Every inch of my body was stiff and sore. *God.* I exercised regularly, but I was going to have to adopt a serious workout regimen to prepare for next year. Slowly, I stretched out the worst aches and dragged myself to the shower, where I stood under the hot pulse of the massager until the skin on my fingertips shriveled.

The scent of coffee greeted me when I emerged, hair wet and wrapped in a robe. I followed the fragrance to the kitchen, where Erik was setting a take-out tray with two coffee cups and a paper bag on the counter. Either he kept a change of clothes in his truck or he'd driven to his loft here in the city, because he hadn't been wearing those jeans and that flannel shirt when he'd come through my door last night.

For an endless moment I just looked at him, unable to say a word. My chest was tight, my heart *so* full. The sex had been amazing, but a million orgasms were nothing compared to the sweet joy of knowing that he was here or the memory of the way he'd kissed me earlier.

As if he needed me. Not just needed to fuck me, but needed *me*.

But I'd been so exhausted. Even as he'd made love to me, it had felt like a dream. Now the reality of it all finally swelled over me. Erik was here.

And I was desperately in love with him.

With emotion clogging my throat, I softly greeted him. "Hey."

He glanced up and everything inside me froze. His eyes were cold. Glacial. Just the same pale blue that they'd always been, but I'd seen warmth in that blue gaze before. I'd seen heat and need and more.

Now there was only ice.

He regarded me from across the room with

the same cold indifference that I'd seen in him for months. "You're awake."

I wished that I wasn't. Nodding blindly, trying to conceal the painful hitch of my breath, I looked at my hands and tightened the belt of my robe. My fingers were shaking.

"You're all right?"

"I'm not hurt," I said.

His jaw hardened. Abruptly he turned toward the window overlooking the yard, pushing his hands into the pockets of his jeans. "Do you want to go to the police so that you can press charges?"

Disbelief held me silent for a second. "Against you?"

"Yes."

"No." I couldn't stop my laugh and it felt like a razor in my throat. "God, if I were going to do that, I'd report your father. You should, too. But I don't think it would go over too well when we told them he sent me to your house knowing you suffered from a curse. So I'll just settle for quitting and letting him deal with that fallout."

He glanced at me. "You're leaving the firm?"

"Wouldn't you?"

"Yes." His gaze searched my face. "I'll make sure you have a recommendation. Or get it from

Douglas, if you don't want it from me. You worked for him long enough."

My old boss. "I will."

"Let me know if you have trouble. I'll make calls. But you probably won't need it. There are more than a few local firms that would love to have you on board." His mouth twisted a little. "I'd have tried to bring you in even before my father did, if not for..."

The curse. Right. And I desperately wanted him to go now. Last night hadn't changed anything. This morning hadn't changed anything.

Maybe I'd just dreamed it, after all.

So I simply nodded, my insides filled with brittle ice that was ready to shatter into sharp edges and rip me to shreds.

Expression suddenly haggard, he pushed his hand through his hair and turned away again. "My dad brought D&E into the firm because he realized you'd triggered the curse. He thought if you were always around, you might warm up to me. That I wouldn't have been able to resist pursuing you. But I'd *never* have risked you like that, Olivia."

I knew. But it was cold comfort, because I wanted him enough to take that risk. Yet obviously Erik didn't feel the same. God, I'd been so stupid.

Reading so much into the curse after looking at a single photo of his grandparents. Hoping that it all meant he loved me. My instincts had screamed that he was the one and I'd foolishly listened.

But it had all just been hormones and wishful thinking. Again.

"Thanks for trying anyway," I said.

"I should kill him."

His dad? "If you do, you'll probably have a really shitty Christmas."

A short, hollow laugh broke from him. "That's already a given."

Here, too. Then he looked to me, and I prayed that he couldn't see how I was shaking from the tension of holding myself together. Slowly he crossed the kitchen, his gaze intense—and the blue was warmer now, but it didn't matter. I already knew what was coming next. He might use different words, but it would all mean the same thing.

Good-bye, Olivia.

He stopped close enough to touch, but my arms were wrapped around my middle. His throat worked before he spoke. "I think you're amazing, Olivia. So incredible. I'm sorry you were caught in this. I should have done a better job protecting you."

It wasn't his fault any more than it was mine.

But I couldn't take any more of this. Every apology was a knife in my chest, a reminder of how much he regretted all of this—and of how he'd wished that he'd never met me.

Jaw tight, I glanced toward the window. Outside, his truck sat in the drive, and remembering the state of my own rig was like spotting a raft of practicality in an ocean of rioting emotion. I jumped onto it before the pain drowned me. "I'll need to make a police report about my Jeep. For the insurance."

A long moment passed before he answered. "Right."

"I'm just going to stick as close to the truth as I can. I'll say I walked up your drive so that you could sign papers and when we came back my rig had been ripped apart. We didn't see anyone do it. Then I was stranded at your lodge until the storm passed."

"All right. I'll say the same." He stepped back and turned away, his gaze dropping to his hands. When he looked up again, the ice had returned. "I arranged to have a car sent here for you. It should arrive this afternoon."

"Thanks." *Go now. Please.*

"And if you need anything else…I'll send you

my lawyer's contact info."

"Your lawyer," I echoed numbly.

"I don't know where I'll be. I'm going to try distance. Maybe Europe. Anywhere that's far enough I can't get to you in one night."

But he didn't have to go. I hadn't been hurt. Maybe he didn't want to be with me but he didn't have to move half the world away. Next year, I could just open my doors again.

I could have Erik for one night. One night a year for the rest of my life.

Knowing he only came because he had no other choice.

Eyes burning, I looked away from him. The Ironwood witch's curse had really, *really* missed its mark. The frost giant wasn't the one being torn apart here.

Agitated all at once, he raked his hand through his hair again and stalked back across the kitchen. "We didn't use protection. If you're pregnant—"

"I'm on birth control," I interrupted before he could say more. Whatever his suggestion, I suspected that I couldn't bear hearing it.

His body suddenly still, Erik nodded. His voice was flat. "That will make it simpler, then."

Simpler. God, was he *trying* to hurt me now?

"So that's everything, right? You didn't leave your spear under the bed?"

His shuttered gaze shot to my face, then away. "That's everything."

"Great," I said. "Thanks."

He nodded, chest lifting on a ragged breath. For an instant he seemed lost, his pale eyes blindly scanning the kitchen until they lit on me, standing in the doorway with my arms wrapped tight around my stomach. Torment filled his gaze.

Desolation lined his face. "I'm so sorry, Olivia."

His regret was a spear of ice through my chest, but there was nothing left to hurt. I was numb now. Frozen.

"Just go," I said and stood unmoving as he went. I stood unmoving as I heard the door close behind him. A long time seemed to pass before I heard his engine start, and when his truck pulled out of the drive, I finally forced myself to the window and watched him go, so that I couldn't pretend later that his leaving had been a dream. Because the reality was right there in my empty driveway. It was right here in my empty kitchen.

He was gone.

Stiffly I moved to the coffee and takeout bag he'd left on the counter—the only remaining sign that he'd been here. I dumped the coffee in the sink. Both cups. He'd bought one for himself, as if he'd intended to eat breakfast with me. Except he'd apparently changed his mind on the way, because his cold indifference had returned before I'd said a word to him. I glanced into the bag and my legs sank out from beneath me.

He'd brought biscuits. Maybe even fluffy ones.

But now they were salty, because the ice inside me shattered, melting into tears and I was nothing but a crying heap on the cold kitchen floor, desperately trying to hold in each harsh sob that ripped from my chest. But they only came harder, no matter how I pressed my hands against my mouth to stop them.

Oh, God. *Oh, God.* I should have known this was coming. My mom had warned me. I should have been prepared.

But there was never any way to prepare for a broken heart.

CHAPTER ELEVEN

ERIK HADN'T JUST ARRANGED FOR A CAR. HE'D outright bought one for me. Less than two hours after he'd gone, a representative from the dealership arrived. He carefully avoided glancing at my puffy face and reddened eyes while I signed the paperwork, and by the time he left, I was in possession of a new Jeep.

Maybe I'd pay Erik back. Maybe I wouldn't. After all, I didn't have a job now, and my mortgage payments weren't going to disappear. My savings would last a while but not forever. And it didn't matter what kind of recommendation my boss wrote—construction was always slow in winter, which meant money was tight. A lot of smaller firms would hold off on hiring anyone until the spring.

So I didn't know what was coming in the next few months. But the arrival of the Jeep forced me to stop crying, and I knew what I had to do over the next few hours.

I emailed John Gulbrandr, resigning effective immediately. After contacting my insurance company, I called the sheriff's office in the town closest to Erik's lodge and reported what had happened to my Jeep, then arranged to call in when I arrived on site so a deputy could meet me there. Finally I texted my mom and let her know that I'd be arriving late.

All of this necessary. Practical. But none of it was as important as the last thing on my list: seeing Erik again. Because I owed him something. Not money. Not a thanks for the Jeep.

I needed to apologize for not shooting him.

It would probably be the most messed-up reason a woman ever apologized to a man. But it needed to be done.

As soon as I packed up the Jeep, I was on the road again. Doubts assaulted me every mile. Emotionally I was a wreck. Chances were that I'd start bawling the second I saw him. I should just meet up with the deputy and drive on. The apology could wait.

Except it couldn't. Not if he was leaving. It wouldn't be the same sending a message through his lawyer.

My chest was a numb, hollow ache by the time I left the highway and started up the road to his place. I slowed as I came upon a snowplow idling farther up—and beyond it, the blacktop was completely cleared of snow.

So this was where Erik had fought the Hound. Trying not to picture the werewolf's terrifying transformation, I carefully eased around the unmoving snowplow.

I passed the big shovel at the front of the plow. Horror clutched my throat and I slammed to a stop.

A frozen pile of blood and fur and flesh lay against the snowbank. I stared at it, fear scraping icy fingers down my spine. Erik had said something about Odin's ravens carrying the body away at dawn, but he hadn't just left it lying in the road. I'd seen him toss it into the snowbank and then cover it. There'd still been some blood visible, but not the body.

The snowplow driver was standing over the frozen mass, shaking his head. When I stopped, he turned to wave me down and began coming my way.

I rolled down the window and freezing air blasted in. The storm was over, but the day was clear and the wind had a knife's edge. The plow driver wore a black stocking cap and a heavy coat, but his cheeks and nose were red from the biting cold.

"It's all right!" the driver called over the noise of his diesel engine, then his voice lowered as he made it to the window of my Jeep. "My plow scraped it out of the snowbank. It looks bad—I about had a heart attack when it tumbled out in front of me—but it's not a person."

What about a werewolf? Uneasy, I studied the bloodied heap. "What is it?"

"A couple of wolves. They've been torn up some, but…" He shook his head. "I don't know what got 'em. Bear or something, maybe come out of hibernation. I heard there was a car farther up the road that was ripped apart during the storm. Maybe if a bear was hungry enough and looking for food, one might do something like that. Maybe it smelled something inside."

"It was my Jeep," I said faintly.

"True?"

I nodded.

"Then you were probably lucky you weren't in it." He huffed out a breath and glanced toward his plow. "I won't keep you. I called this in and now I'm waiting for the sheriff, but I'd rather wait in the cab than in this cold."

"Of course. Watch out for bears," I suggested with a weak smile.

He snorted and stepped back, offering a little salute. I waved and drove on, my heart thundering.

Wolves. Not just the one wolf that had been lying dead on the snowbank, but *wolves*. Buried where Erik had buried the Hound. If Erik had driven this way earlier, it would have still been buried. He might not have realized that Odin's ravens hadn't picked it up, after all.

And last night, when Erik had been fighting, he hadn't just been fighting the Hound. He'd been fighting himself, fighting the curse. Could a trickster's illusion be so effective?

Maybe it could if Erik was tearing apart something that smelled like wolf, bled like wolf—and looked half-human. Why would Erik question it if he'd had blood steaming on his shirt? That hadn't been faked.

My mind racing, remembering how a wolf had dashed in front of the truck before I'd rammed into the Hound—and how a thin arm had disappeared, but a dead wolf had lain in its place—I was almost at Erik's driveway before I realized that the officer from the sheriff's department had already arrived. The patrol vehicle was parked behind my old Jeep and the deputy crouched in the road, taking pictures of the damage.

I pulled into the end of Erik's driveway, blocking the entrance so that I wouldn't block the main road. This wasn't the order I'd hoped to do this. I'd intended to call the sheriff's office as soon as I got here, drive up to Erik's house and apologize, then use the excuse of the deputy's imminent arrival to leave as fast as I could without seeming to run away.

Maybe this was better, though. After seeing that frozen bloodied heap in the road, I might be having a longer conversation with Erik that I'd intended. I had to warn him that the Hound might not be dead. Because the only reason the Hound would fake his death was so that it'd be easier to ambush Erik later.

God. Maybe he already had?

I cast my gaze up the winding drive, then jumped when a tap sounded at my window. The deputy. So worried about Erik, I'd almost forgotten about him.

Erik *had* to be fine. I'd get this done as fast as possible and go warn him. Grabbing my coat and hat, I stepped out into the bitter cold.

"Thanks for coming," I told the deputy. "I'm Olivia Martin—I called this in. That's my rig."

"Ben Tooley." With a tilt of his head, he gestured for me to walk with him. Though blond, he had a bit of an Andy Griffith vibe, complete with a long, lanky walk and easy smile. "You say you called this in?"

"I did. A couple of hours ago, and made a report to the deputy on duty."

"Ah. The last shift. I was rolling by and saw it— lucky for both of us, I guess, since now I won't be sent back out here and you won't have to wait." The deputy stopped at the side of my Jeep, studying the claw marks ripping through the door panel. His low whistle joined the shake of his head. "Big, whatever it was. Did you see who did it?"

"No." Already feeling the cold, I shoved my bare hands into my coat pockets, and stuck with the story. "I was taking papers up to the Gulbrandrs' lodge to be signed. When Mr. Gulbrandr walked me back down, we found it like this."

He glanced at the shattered glass. "And you didn't hear anything?"

"No. But I was in his house for a few minutes. So it must have happened then."

"Was anything stolen?"

"I don't know. Some of the clothes from my suitcase were tossed around, I guess. But I didn't get close enough to look through and see if anything else was touched. I figured that if something big enough to do that was hanging out in the woods, then I'd be better off back at the lodge."

"You probably thought right." Tooley glanced toward Erik's driveway. "Is Mr. Gulbrandr home now?"

"Yes." Or I assumed he was. I hadn't really questioned that he'd return here—his front door was shattered, and even if Odin's ravens had collected the snake's body, there was a hell of a mess to clean up in the tower room.

The deputy nodded. "Well, I've got enough pictures already. I'd like to head up and take his statement, then return to record the list of items still inside and those missing. No offense, but I can't leave you here with the damaged property until we've determined if anything has been stolen." This time, his friendly smile was rueful. "I know that anyone driving by could have grabbed something out of these broken windows, but regulations are regulations."

"It's okay." A relief, actually. We'd be heading

up to Erik's place and I could make sure he was all right—maybe even tell him about the Hound if we had a second of privacy. "So you'll follow me up?"

He looked back at his patrol rig. "If you don't mind me hitching a short ride, I can leave my truck there, and there'd be less chance of someone messing with yours."

There was already zero chance, given the lack of traffic on this road. Of course, with the Hound still out there somewhere, Tooley might come back to find it in the same state as my old Jeep.

"You aren't worried *that* will happen to it while you're gone?" I cast a significant glance at the claw marks.

A laughing grin split his face, as if that was the funniest thing he'd heard all day. "I think it'll be all right."

"It's fine with me, then." The faster we went, the faster I'd stop worrying about Erik. I climbed into my Jeep—Tooley was already at the passenger door, swinging it open. *Crap.* I'd expected that he'd have to call this in first and that it would be a minute or so before we were on our way. I snatched my heavy shoulder bag off the passenger seat to make room for him. "Sorry."

"No worries." He breathed deep as he settled in.

"New?"

"Yeah. I'm assuming the insurance will write off the other one as totaled."

Awkwardly, I tried to fit my bag on the console between us. I could put it in the back, but I didn't want to twist around with my giant bag while he was in that seat—I'd probably whack him. I settled for slinging the strap over my shoulder and holding the bag on my lap like a baby. It was only a quarter mile.

I started up the drive. The heater was welcome on my face, though Tooley didn't look as if the biting air and wind chill had affected him at all. He'd been out taking pictures for a while, yet there wasn't a hint of red on his nose. I couldn't say the same, but I was glad of it. When Erik saw me, I could blame the redness and puffiness on the cold. He didn't need to know that I'd spent part of the afternoon bawling.

And something really, *really* wasn't right.

My gut was tight, my instincts screaming. My fingers clenched on the wheel but I tried not to let my sudden unease bleed into my voice. "I just realized—I should have mentioned this. On my way up, I came across a snowplow that had stopped because it ran into a little pack of frozen wolves. The driver thought a bear must have gotten to them."

Frowning, Tooley slowly nodded. "Maybe a bear."

"But he said he'd called it in and was waiting for a deputy. So I don't know if you want to take care of that first before we run an inventory through my rig."

He nodded again. "I'll radio in and see if they've sent anyone else when we get back. From what it sounds like, Gulbrandr saw as little as you did, so the statement shouldn't take more than a minute or two."

"Great." I forced a smile and kept my eyes fixed on the road. Was my gun still in my bag?

No. Oh, *shit*. I'd left it in the nightstand by my bed.

And what if I was wrong? What if I was just freaking out because I knew the Hound was out there somewhere, and my instincts were off? What was I going to do, shoot a deputy?

After quitting my job and losing the man I loved, going to jail for the rest of my life would just be the sweet cherry on top.

My relief was a solid, thumping beat in my chest as Erik's fortress came into view. I'd been right. He was back. His truck sat near the gatehouse, where a hanging sheet of clear plastic told me he'd already begun working on sealing up the house and fixing the front door.

The portcullis still worked. If I could get into the house and lower it, I'd be okay.

"How did you figure it out?"

My blood froze. I glanced at Tooley—not Tooley anymore, but a man with silver hair and yellow eyes.

His smile was sharp as he leaned closer, as if sharing a confidence. "I can hear your heart pounding, you know. I can smell the stink of your fear. So tell me what gave me away."

Now that I was sure, a few things were shouting at me. "You said 'who.'" My voice was a terrified rasp. "When asking if I saw what tore up my rig, you said 'who' instead of 'what,' even though those were obviously claw marks. And you didn't check in before coming up to the house. Any real deputy would have checked in before entering a private residence, just in case something happened."

"Ah. Shoddy work. You surprised me, though. I'd only intended to take the registration from your glove box so that I'd have your home address. When I heard you coming, I had to improvise. I thought you'd noticed the patrol vehicle wasn't real." His grimace revealed fangs and pointed teeth. "Was there anything else?"

"Your nose wasn't red, even though you'd been out in the cold. God. You don't have to do this. Just go home."

"All right."

Stopping the Jeep behind Erik's truck, I stared at the Hound in surprise. "You will?"

"After he's dead. I have three brothers to avenge. Nothing will steer me from this course—and it will be so much more satisfying than killing him when he isn't aware of anything but your cunt. Now he'll know what real pain is." A terrible grin widened his mouth. "So do you think you can make it to the gatehouse?"

I sure as hell was going to try. My fingers flew to the door handle and I threw myself out of my seat, knees cushioned by the snow.

He was on me before I made it to my feet. Long fingers caught my neck in a chokehold. I tried to scream Erik's name and only a wheeze emerged, my windpipe cut off, my lungs already aching as my panicking body tried to suck in more air.

A snout covered in human skin nuzzled my cheek. "There, now. Here he comes. I don't even think he knows we're here yet."

Terror and pain filled my eyes with burning

tears. Desperately I blinked them away as Erik stepped through the plastic sheeting, his expression drawn, the deep shadows on his face making his features appear gaunt. He moved with the stiff, broken gait of someone in terrible agony, as if even breathing hurt.

Then he glanced up and it all changed. He stood utterly still, his jaw like steel, his eyes diamond. My warrior. His glittering gaze caught mine across the distance.

The Hound spoke against my ear, loud enough that Erik had to hear. "He's probably wondering if this is real or a trick. So how should we convince him?" Clawed fingers dug into my hip and he ground his pelvis against my back. "After last night, he'll probably recognize every sound you make as you're held down and fucked."

Though he didn't move, Erik's face whitened. Tears burned over my cheeks and I struggled against the Hound, sick with sudden rage. It had to be an empty threat—raping me would make him as vulnerable as the curse was supposed to have made Erik—but if he was going to hurt me to torture Erik, then he should just get on with it. This was just drawing it out, because I knew Erik didn't dare take a step toward me, not while the Hound held me like this. And nothing I did mattered, not kicking or scratching, because he healed in an instant, and my gun was so, so far out of reach.

But my bag was still hanging across my shoulder, the big pouch lying against my stomach. In it was everything I needed to keep from starving or freezing or being eaten by bears.

Or ripped apart by a Hound.

Still kicking, weakly I flailed back at him with my right hand. My left hand crept into my bag.

Erik didn't look down, didn't give me away. Instead he focused on the Hound. "Let her go. She has nothing to do with this."

"She has *everything* to do with this, son of Odin's son." A deep growl rumbled against my back. His breath was hot on my cheek. "When you see her dead, you'll know the pain that drives me now. But not for long. You have no spear and you'll soon follow her."

Oh, God. *Hurry, hurry.* Where the hell was it?

Hope burst through me as my desperately searching fingers brushed a smooth steel canister. I felt for the grip—oh, thank God, it wasn't hair-spray—and flipped open the safety top with my thumb.

Suddenly I stopped flailing, my gaze locked

on Erik's, my breath coming in thin, wheezing sobs. I let my knees sag, as if I couldn't hold myself up anymore. The Hound adjusted his grip on my throat—loosening very slightly.

Holding my breath, closing my eyes, I brought the pepper spray up beside my face and shot it blindly behind me.

A gurgling screech pierced my ear. Pain ripped the side of my throat as the Hound reeled back, claws dragging over my skin, but I was free, stumbling into the snow. I didn't breathe, didn't open my eyes, just scrambled forward, my knees whacking into my bag as I crawled as fast as I could. The Hound was shrieking, a ululating howl of agony. *Burn, you fucker.* It didn't matter how fast he healed. The pepper spray wouldn't instantly dissipate—it probably felt like he was being sprayed again and again.

With a fleshy *thunk*, the howl cut short. I glanced back then wished I hadn't. Erik hadn't used a wooden spear. A giant icicle had been shoved through the Hound's nightmarish jaws as if it had tried to swallow a thick pole. My head swam, and I shut my eyes again as Erik reached for those jaws, but the wet rip of flesh and bone made my stomach heave into my throat. I was still crawling, I realized then, and tried to get to my feet, but my head was spinning and I couldn't breathe.

Strong arms swept me up. A deep voice said my name. But it was too late.

Holy shit. I was going to faint.

CHAPTER TWELVE

PAIN STUNG THE SIDE OF MY NECK. I JERKED upward and almost cracked my forehead against Erik's jaw. He was leaning over me. Vaulted ceilings arched above him. I was lying on a cushion.

The sofa. In his great room.

"You're safe, Olivia." His deep voice was low, soothing. "I'm just cleaning the scratch on your neck."

From the Hound's claws. Memory swamped me. Oh, God.

I fell back against the cushion again. "Is he dead?"

"Yes."

"For sure this time?"

"Yes." His smile was strained, but his fingers were gentle as he swept a peroxide-soaked cottonball over my skin. I hissed at the sting. "You were brilliant."

The pepper spray. "I was desperate."

"You saved us."

"I only distracted him. You finished it." My throat was a solid ache. "I was coming to tell you that he'd tricked us last night. That you'd just been fighting his wolves. A plow scraped them out of the snowbank. But he was already at my Jeep and it wasn't until we were driving up here that I realized…"

My breath shuddered and I couldn't continue. I didn't need to.

Erik nodded, his thumb tracing the line of my jaw. His eyes were warm as they searched my face. "You're all right now?"

I'm not hurt, I almost said. But I was. My chest still hollow. My heart shredded.

And I still owed him. Stiffly I nodded, then sat up. Erik withdrew his hand and stood, fists shoving into his pockets. The pain in my chest deepened. "I didn't know about the wolves until I was almost here. I just wanted to say…I'm sorry that I didn't shoot you."

His pale blue gaze shot to mine. White suddenly edged his mouth.

"Not that I want to," I hastened to explain. "I just... You made a choice. I made a promise and didn't keep it, never had any *intention* of keeping it, because I'd made another choice. And this whole thing is fucked up, so I end up being sorry for not shooting you—sorry I didn't respect your choice. But I'm *not* sorry I didn't really shoot you."

His eyes closed. "You came here to apologize to me?"

"Yes. And no. That's why it's fucked up." I hauled in a shaking breath. "I can't imagine how you felt, coming through that door. Expecting me to stop you and not."

"Like a fucking monster," he said hoarsely.

Tears stinging my eyes, I could only nod. "I'm sorry for that."

"Don't be. Jesus. You had no good choice, Olivia. I know that."

"I know you didn't, either. I guess it worked out as best as it possibly could." Except my heart had been shattered. "But when I came into the kitchen this afternoon and you looked at me like that, like you just couldn't stand being near me, I thought you might hate me for failing to do what I'd promised."

"No." He regarded me as if stunned. "God, Olivia. I couldn't."

"Then *why*? Obviously you meant to stay a little while longer. But then you were just ice."

"Jesus. That wasn't—" Raking his hands through his hair, Erik abruptly turned away, but not before I saw the torment in his face. His voice was flat when he continued, "I heard you coming down the hall. I didn't know how you… I decided to wait and see how you reacted when you realized I was there. But you didn't even come into the kitchen. You were just cringing by the door, and I—"

"Felt like a monster again?" When his eyes closed, I knew I'd struck the mark. God. Had he misread so much? "I wasn't cringing. I just wasn't expecting you to go cold on me. After last night, it was a slap in the face for you to freeze me out."

"I didn't mean— I wasn't freezing you out. I wasn't trying to hurt you." His expression tortured, he faced me again. "I was just trying to hold it together. Trying to take care of what needed to be taken care of, knowing I needed to go."

So I'd misread him, too. "But you *don't* have to go. It was good last night, wasn't it? And this morning."

"*Good?*" He shook his head, but it wasn't a denial.

Instead his gaze seemed haunted as he scanned my face. "Yes. It was...good."

That was the understatement of the year. "And I wasn't hurt. So maybe dinner next week?"

He stared at me for a long second. "A date?"

"Yeah." I shrugged, hoping that the casual gesture would conceal the way my hands were clenched so tightly that my fingers ached, and my heart was pounding out of my chest. "I have some free time. Because I just, you know, quit my job."

Eyes suddenly bleak, he shook his head. "I can't."

"Okay. Then what time is good for you?"

"I can't, Olivia."

This time it was harsh, abrupt, and I battled to keep my response light, wishing that I would just shut up, just stop, but I couldn't. "Why? The danger's gone. I wasn't hurt and it all turned out okay. There's no reason for you to move to Europe."

"Not this month. But in the future? The curse isn't just for this year, but *every* year. Is the next guy you date going to be understanding when I show up at your door?"

"The next guy I date?" I echoed stupidly. Why would I date anyone else?

"Or when you get married, have kids." He

turned away, fists balled at his sides, his shoulders rigid. "What are you going to tell your husband?"

My husband. Wow. He was moving really fast. I hadn't even invited him to Christmas dinner yet.

But I'd been heading in that direction, I realized. I'd pictured myself moving toward forever... with him. But when Erik imagined the future, he saw me with someone else.

"Okay, well." I didn't know what was holding me together now. I wished I had even a little bit of his ice, but my throat was burning, my eyes were burning. "I guess that's that. Have a nice life."

I heard his ragged breath, saw his nod out of the corner of my eye, but I didn't stop to say more. I grabbed up my bag and walked as fast as I could to the door. Not even the door. Just plastic, and as I passed out of the gatehouse heavy drops fell on my cheeks. Not tears, but icy drops.

The big icicles hanging from the eaves were melting, and I thanked God for them, because if my tears did start falling before I got out of here I could use the icicles as an excuse. My whole body was shaking, my legs feeling too weak to carry me out to my Jeep, yet I made it somehow, then realized that all of the bloodied snow and the Hound's body were gone.

I climbed into my seat and started the engine, but didn't even try to put it in gear. My breath was coming in burning shudders and I'd probably ram into a tree. I just had to wait. Pain went away. It always did. I'd gotten along without him for eighteen months. I could survive the rest of my life.

My teeth clenched, and I sucked in another breath. God. It would help if Erik went back into the house. But he'd followed me out and was standing at the entrance to the gatehouse, his eyes cold, his face desolate. No shoes, no coat. Idiot.

Not that it mattered. The house had been cold inside, too. No fire, no heat. No wonder he was frozen through. No wonder his heart was a fucking block of ice.

Except…the icicles were melting. Even though the temperature was cold enough to bite.

My sobbing breaths suddenly quieted and I stared at him through the windshield. No heat inside the house.

The warmth had to be coming from somewhere, though. This fortress had snow and ice piled all around it, but the icicles told me that heat was leaking through. A *lot* of heat. And here Erik was, a freaking frost giant who could control snow and ice, who seemed just as cold from the outside.

But something inside him *must* be burning, because the icicles were dripping like tears.

And he'd believed that I'd seen him as a monster. Not a warrior. Not a man I admired.

I'd never told him he was. He'd told me so many times that I was amazing and brave. I'd never said anything remotely similar, because I'd been so busy remembering how he'd hurt me that I hadn't let myself be vulnerable again.

At least, not my heart. I'd risked my body. I'd told him I wanted him, but I held every other emotion close to my chest. I hadn't told him that I love him—all because I wasn't really certain how he felt about me.

He must be even less certain of my feelings. And maybe a worse torment than the curse was having someone you loved so close and believing that they didn't love you back...and that there was no chance that they'd *ever* love you back. Only a few hours ago, Erik had looked at me with ice in his eyes and had ripped my heart out. When I looked at him and hid everything I felt, when I shrugged and pretended that none of this mattered, maybe I didn't leave his heart in any better shape.

Now he was coming toward me, a concerned frown creasing his brow. No wonder. I'd been sitting here a long time.

I rolled down the window. "I was going to point out that you need better insulation, because those giant icicles are going to kill someone. But I guess they already did."

That startled a laugh from him. God, I wanted to kiss him. Was this instincts? Hormones?

I didn't care anymore. Maybe I was mistaken. But I'd take that risk.

Opening the door, I slid out of the car. "It's a really shitty curse, Erik."

His amusement died. "I know."

"No, not because of what it does to you—it's just a shitty curse. Just like you have shitty insulation. It's crap. Because a thousand years ago women were basically like cattle. So what kind of curse is that? A frost giant rapes some random woman, but no one would care except her family. She's got no rights. It hurts the girl more than it ever hurts him."

His eyes were haunted again. "Yes."

"Well, *you* think so, because this is the twenty-first century and you're a decent guy. A thousand years ago, they probably weren't so decent. Your ancestors were probably all, 'I have to stick my dick in some wench, but who cares? That's what women are for!' So how would that hurt the guy? Unless it wasn't the act itself that was the curse, but the woman he did it to."

"Olivia—"

"I mean, it's not *practical*, right?" I stalked closer to him and his body seemed to tighten with my every step. "And, okay, maybe you don't curse someone unless you're really pissed, but when you do, you make sure it's practical. You make sure it really hurts someone. So you force him to hurt his mother, his sister. Or the woman he loves."

Erik abruptly stilled, his tormented gaze locked on mine.

"Do you?" I could hardly breathe. "Do you love me?"

His eyes closed in defeat. "It doesn't change anything."

I was suddenly light. So light. "Yes, it does. It changes everything."

"No."

"If it didn't matter, you wouldn't have concealed it from me." And love always mattered. That was why I'd hidden mine from him.

"I can't bear—"

"What? To be around me? Or you don't want to hurt me?" I laughed. "God, you know that's shit. My mom can be our early warning system. Or maybe you're just going to decide for me, huh? Play the big strong frost giant and don't let me choose whether to take risks or not."

"Jesus. Of all people, Olivia, I'd trust you to weigh risk and make decisions. You saved us both last night." Misery bracketed his mouth in deep lines. "But you want a date, Olivia. I want—"

"Forever?"

Yearning filled his gaze. "Yes. God help me, yes."

"What if I want that, too?"

"If I could make you love me?" The agonized longing on his face stopped my heart. "If I thought... it was possible. If you weren't afraid of me."

My mouth dropped open. "You think I'm *afraid* of you?"

"I think you tried not to be." Remembered pain filled his eyes. "But I saw how you looked at me after I killed the serpent, Olivia. You were terrified."

"Of the snake! Not of you. And remember, I *shot* the snake. Was I nervous when you came into my bedroom? Sure. But if I'd been anywhere near terrified, I'd have shot you, too." I drew in a long breath. "What if I want to stay?"

His gaze froze on my face again. His voice was hoarse. "I can't ask you to."

"Then tell me to go."

"You should."

"Then tell me to. But know I want forever. Know that I love you, too." Tears suddenly trembled in my eyes, my voice. "So tell me to go, Erik. Tell me it doesn't change anything, knowing that you'll rip my heart out. And if you don't want me to stay, I won't ever ask again. I swear I'll never ask you again."

A promise that was so close to the one he'd made this morning. *I swear I'll never touch you again.* Both of us, making promises we couldn't bear to keep.

He broke his in the next second, catching my face in his big hands and capturing my mouth in a desperate kiss. Winding my arms around his neck, I pressed closer, joy bursting in my chest and raining tears down my cheeks. Happiness was supposed to make me stop crying, but I couldn't.

"God, Olivia," he said roughly against my lips. "I can't let you go again."

"You won't need to."

"But you need to know." His hands buried in my hair, his mouth trailing kisses over my jaw and down to my throat before he lifted his head with a harsh groan. "You need to know. The frost giant isn't a different man. That's all me. Just…without control. And I want you under me all the time,

Olivia. To be inside you, feeling you shatter around me. Not once a year. That's just when I can't control it. But the way it was last night—that's how it will be with me."

Hard, relentless, and excruciatingly tender. My heart so full, I smiled up at him. "Do you think I just took everything you gave because I had no choice? That wasn't some martyr lying there. That was *me*, loving it all."

And loving his kiss now, the warm stroke of his tongue—and the shock of cold that followed when he licked my neck. I laughed, shivering against him in surprise and swift pleasure.

"Show off," I said.

His grin was so gorgeous, and I was sorry that it faded so quickly. Gravel filled his voice. "I was so terrified that I would hurt you."

"Your grandmother was okay."

"But not every woman was. Do you think I'd have been so worried if they'd all made it through all right? Some of have been injured; others killed themselves afterward. And my grandmother already knew that side of my grandfather. There was no surprise. I had no idea you'd be familiar with any kind of magic. But even though you were, if you'd changed your mind, if you'd been afraid…"

With his size and strength, he'd have hurt me. Very badly. "So we were lucky."

"Yes. And it could still happen. You have to realize that, Olivia. If you're sick on the solstice or just not in the mood or if you're pregnant—"

I stopped him before he could get any further. "Early warning system," I reminded him. "Okay? If my mom thinks something could go wrong, I take a flight out a few days before. And we'll just always buy a ticket in advance, every year."

Though his jaw was tight, he nodded. "It's practical."

Of course it was. "And same goes for the Hounds," I told him. "More might show up. But we'll be prepared, okay? Because I'm always prepared."

"Thank God." His fingers tenderly traced the line of my jaw. "If you were ever hurt, I wouldn't want to take another breath."

"Though I'm the worst thing to ever happen to you?" I could tease him now. "Even though you wished you'd never met me?"

"The best was meeting you. The worst was knowing I might hurt you if I fell in love." He kissed me again and then said, "That was all it took. A kiss. It hit me so fast and you were so calm. Like you didn't care that I'd walked away. So I thought I'd stopped it in time. That I could at least save you."

"By backing off?"

"Yes."

"But you fell anyway, even though we barely spoke off the job. Why didn't you suspect that I would, too?"

His teeth nipped my bottom lip. "I thought you'd be too practical."

"No." Laughing, I shook my head, then gasped as he swept me off my feet. God, I could get used to this—and my instincts had been *so* right. Erik was definitely, absolutely, the one. I linked my arms around his neck. "Speaking of impractical decisions, you're out of a job and I'm out of a job. We should start up a firm together. M&G Engineering."

"That's practical."

"My reason isn't. I'm crazy about you. I want to be with you all the time," I said. "And I want what you want, starting with building my own firm with a brilliant partner who isn't an asshole. I want the same things you'd have wished for, if you didn't have to worry about the curse."

He stopped suddenly, his arms tightening around me. "Olivia."

It was all he said, but his voice was rough with emotion, his eyes diamond.

"Erik." Softly I kissed him. "I know the curse weighs on you. I know the whole thing is fucked up. But in all of it, this is one thing that's absolutely right. And it's not a risk for me. The risk is not having you, because I'm pretty sure that love is the only thing that can hurt so much—or feel so amazing. The curse doesn't come close."

Throat working, he nodded and continued inside the house. "Tell me what else you want, Olivia."

That was easy. "You. Love. Maybe a family, one day."

"The usual, then."

Exactly that. Just the usual. With a cursed frost giant.

"I hope you fixed the chimneys," I said, then laughed until he kissed me again.

THE END

ABOUT THE AUTHOR

Meljean was raised in the middle of the woods, and hid under her blankets at night with fairy tales, comic books, and romances. She left the forest and went on a misguided tour through the world of accounting before focusing on her first loves, reading and writing–and she realized that monsters, superheroes, and happily-ever-afters are easily found between the covers, as well as under them, so she set out to make her own.

Meljean also writes as fantasy romance author Milla Vane. For more information, a full list of titles, and excerpts, please visit:

www.meljeanbrook.com

CPSIA information can be obtained
at www.ICGtesting.com
Printed in the USA
LVHW101338290422
717462LV00016BB/80

9 781490 503097